Welcome to the wonderful world of Regency Romance!
For a free short story and to listen to me read the first
chapter of all my other Regencies, please go to my website:
https://romancenovelsbyglrobinson.com
or use the QR code:

Thank you!

GL Robinson

The Lord and the Red-Headed Hornet

A Regency Romance

By

GL Robinson

As always, in memory of
my dear sister, Francine.
And for my own twins,
Andy and Claire.

With thanks to my Beta readers,
who keep me on the straight and narrow.

And with thanks to Thomas E. Burch and
CS for their patient technical help.

Cover art: GL Robinson. Designed with Midjourney, 2023.

Contents

Chapter One

"Oh! Good heavens! I'm so sorry!" Amelia looked into the startled face of the gentleman in front of her. He was regarding her with a quizzical expression and laughter in his eyes.

"Seeing you so engrossed in… what is it?" he replied, flicking a corner of the newspaper she was holding, "… The Times, I stepped aside to avoid you, but you chose the same moment to veer off your path and straight into me. I couldn't avoid you, I'm afraid." He smiled apologetically.

It was true. Her eyes had been riveted on the address in the paper in front of her and, without looking up; she had turned down the street it was on. The place she wanted was indeed in this direction but so, it now appeared, was this gentleman. She had walked straight into him.

He was dressed, she could tell, in the height of fashion. He wore a spotless tall hat with a curly brim and an ankle-length pale grey wool driving cloak with many shoulder capes and large silver buttons. It was open over a darker grey fitted coat, a herringbone waistcoat, and smooth buff pantaloons. These were encased below the knee in Hessians polished to such a shine it positively hurt one's eyes to look at them. She wondered what her brother Aurelius would say if he saw them. He had done everything in his power and in the power of old Gibbons who served as general factotum and valet to achieve such a gloss, but without success.

But the gentleman was addressing her. He tipped his hat with his cane and gave her a slight bow.

"Edward Woodbridge, Ma'am, at your service."

If her view of him had instantly assured her of his claim to fashion, his of her did just the opposite. He saw in front of him a woman of above average height, dressed very plainly in a navy-blue pelisse and a matching but rather uncompromising bonnet. In fact, bonnet was not really the word, he decided. It was a very plain hat, with neither feather nor flower to relieve its dullness. However, some lucky impulse had persuaded the wearer to turn up the brim across the front, and it was this that saved it. For the turned-up brim revealed the wayward curls of what was obviously a mass of fiery red hair and a pair of nut-brown eyes, eyes that were now regarding him very candidly.

"Amelia Moreton," said the owner of the eyes, moving her reticule and the newspaper into her left hand in order to extend to him the right. He was surprised. A woman had never offered to shake his hand before. But took it and held it for a moment.

"How may I be of service?" asked Mr. Woodbridge, asking himself why on earth he did so. Why didn't he simply leave this female to her business and go on with his own? "You're too susceptible to a pair of brown eyes, my boy," he said sternly to himself. But it was too late.

"Oh, do you think you could?" said Miss Moreton, looking at him appraisingly. "I'm looking for the home of the Earl of Ailesbury. Do you happen to know where it is?" She looked down the row of stately townhomes of Albemarle Street that lay before her.

Mr. Woodbridge cursed silently. Now he was sure he should have gone on his way. But he answered politely, "Why yes, it's number 23. Just down here on the right. But I'm afraid you will find the Earl from home."

2

"Do you know him then?" asked Miss Moreton. "I'm hoping to see him. Is he nice?"

"I do know him well, as a matter of fact," he replied. "As to whether he is nice, it's not really for me to say, though I find him very nice indeed. You see, I am he."

"You!" said Miss Moreton in evident disbelief. "But I thought him a much older man!"

"Perhaps you mean my father. If so, I'm sorry to inform you he died four years ago."

Miss Moreton ignored this sad loss to the Earl's family. "Anyway, you said your name was Woodbridge. Edward Woodbridge."

"It is. I'm Edward Woodbridge, Earl of Ailesbury, third Baron of Mayne. Perhaps you see why I prefer to simplify it. May I ask why you are looking for me?"

"It's the job, you see," said Miss Moreton, who seemed to have reconciled herself to both his name and his age. "I want to see him... you, I mean, in answer to the advertisement for the job." When he still looked puzzled, she added, "The job of secretary to his... your lordship."

Light dawned on the gentleman in front of her. "But the job of secretary is for a man!"

"It doesn't say that here. Look! It only says His Lordship the Earl of Ailesbury seeks a secretary. The candidate must be well organized and accustomed to working independently. And it gives the address and today's date. There is no mention of gender. I am well organized and I prefer to work independently. If you'd wanted a man, you should have said so." Miss Moreton sounded increasingly indignant. "Anyway, even though I'm not a man, I'm sure I can do it just as well as one. Probably better."

His lordship looked at her for a moment then burst out laughing. "It was my present secretary who wrote the notice for the Times, not I. He is leaving almost immediately for a diplomatic post abroad and I daresay he was a little distrait when he composed it. And I imagine he never considered the possibility of a woman applying for the job. No more did I. But you're right. Why not? You can probably do it as well or better than he." He reached inside his jacket, took out a pocket book, withdrew a card, scribbled a note on it and gave it to her. "Here, he's in the house now. Take this to him and tell him I said to engage you." He tipped his cane to his hat and gave a slight bow. "Good day to you, Miss Moreton. No doubt I shall see you again before long."

He walked jauntily down the street, leaving her standing in astonishment behind him.

Chapter Two

Pulling herself together, Miss Moreton walked swiftly down to number 23 Albemarle Street, mounted the front steps and pulled the bell firmly. It was answered after a moment by a portly gentleman whose attire and demeanor proclaimed him the butler.

"I am Amelia Moreton, here to see his lordship's secretary," she said and thrust the scribbled card into his hand.

If he was surprised first at seeing an unattended young woman at his lordship's door and then at having a very recognizable gilt-edged card pushed unceremoniously upon him, he betrayed it by not so much an eyebrow.

"Yes, Miss… er… Moreton. If you would be so good as to step this way," he said impassively, and led her into what was obviously the library.

"May I bring you some refreshment, Miss Moreton?" intoned the butler.

"Yes, a cup of tea would be most welcome, thank you," she replied, stripping off her gloves and looking around in a business-like fashion.

"At once, Madam," came the solemn reply. "I shall first ask Mr. Wilson to step this way." He left the room in cat-like silence, unexpected for a man of his girth.

A few minutes later, a harassed looking man of about twenty-five came in, holding the gilt-edged card by his fingertips, as if it were red-hot. He was quite short, shorter than Amelia. His fair hair was thinning and he wore a pair of round spectacles clipped to his nose and attached to his lapel by a long black ribbon.

"Miss Moreton?" he said with some hesitation, before giving her brief bow, "I am Clive Wilson, his lordship's secretary." He looked at the tall woman in front of him, an almost martial light in her eye. "This is most irregular. One might almost think his lordship was... er... a trifle...."

"Tipsy?" suggested the lady with a questioning tilt to her chin. "Is he often in that condition so early in the day? I assure you he was not when I saw him not ten minutes ago. Unless," she added fairly, "unless he carries his drink remarkably well."

"No, yes... that is... I mean...," the young man removed his spectacles and began polishing them frantically with a large white handkerchief drawn from his pocket. "I don't quite understand...."

"Why what does it say?" she whisked the card from his fingers. Her upbringing had prevented her from reading the card before delivering it to its intended recipient, but now he had seen it, she felt no such compunction. "Hire her", she read. This elliptical message was followed by a scrawl in which the word Ailesbury could just about be discerned. "It seems quite clear to me. You are told to hire me. Anyway, that is what his lordship directed me to tell you."

"Yes, but ...but ...," the secretary seemed to have difficulty enunciating his misgivings.

Miss Moreton helped him. "You are no doubt astonished his lordship should engage a woman as his secretary. But the fault is your own. You didn't mention a required gender in here." She thrust the newspaper at him. "You only talk about the qualities the person must possess. Well, I possess them and his lordship saw no impediment to taking me on. Now," she walked briskly to the door, "be so kind as to show me my office and apprise me of my duties." She stopped. "But before that, tell me, what is your salary? His lordship said nothing of the matter."

"But... but," stammered the secretary again, aghast at being asked so personal a question by a complete stranger, "even if his lordship is serious, which, Miss Moreton, please give me leave to doubt, his lordship being a man of... odd quirks, you surely do not imagine he will pay you the same as a man?"

"Why ever not? If I do the same work, with I daresay, a greater degree of competence than you, to judge from what was obviously an oversight in the formulation of this advertisement, why should I not be paid the same? And if this is one of his lordship's odd quirks as you term it, you may be assured he will soon be made to understand it is not one I appreciate. Besides, I don't believe it. He seemed reasonable enough."

The poor man, with three years of his lordship's reasonableness under his belt, could give no answer to this. He muttered, "His lordship is generous enough to pay me £60 per annum, £15 per quarter."

"My goodness! That is generous. Yes, that is quite satisfactory. Oh! Run and tell the butler to bring the tea to your office, if you please. He is probably on his way as we speak."

Thoroughly alarmed by this forceful young woman, the secretary unquestioningly did as he was told. He then led her to his office, where tea was soon brought in. Miss Moreton removed her hat and displayed, as the Earl had guessed, a mass

7

of bright red hair. She quickly poured them both a cup of tea, saying they could drink and work at the same time.

There was soon no doubt that everything one was accustomed to think about red hair and temperament was fully displayed in Miss Moreton. She drank tea and ate a number of small pastries with perfect efficiency, while going over the monthly and quarterly accounts that formed the largest part of the secretary's workload. She grasped the facts and figures with amazing rapidity and gave ready expression to her feelings.

"£5 a quarter for candles? What do they do here? Eat them?" she cried, soon followed by, "and £15 for coal? Good heavens! How many people live in this house?"

"Well," stammered the unhappy young man, "his lordship, of course, Mr. Bullock the butler, Mrs. Hancock the housekeeper, Antoine the chef, and perhaps four each of maids and footmen. Most of the stable hands live in the mews. I imagine there is some coal consumption there. But I think that's all."

"I can't imagine the maids, footmen and stable hands enjoy the luxury of a fire in their rooms. So," she did a mental calculation, "that may be eight or nine fireplaces if one includes all his lordship's living accommodations, plus the coal for cooking. At seven shillings and six pence a ton, that is a very great deal of coal for a house of this size! I wonder if his lordship is aware of this?"

Mr. Wilson was very sure that if the Earl had retained any idea of these figures presented to him faithfully every quarter, which he very much doubted, he didn't give a damn about a single one of them. It was his habit to sign without reading drafts in payment of any bill. Often and again he would cry, "sign it yourself, dear boy!" when his secretary tried in vain to catch him as he was going out of the door to the races, to another sporting event, to a party or simply to his club. The fact was, the Earl was so very wealthy these things were of no significance to him at all. Mr. Wilson said none of this to Miss Moreton. He was glad, however, since he was a man who assiduously avoided confrontation, that he would not be around to see the inevitable explosion when she tried to force a serious discussion on a man who took nothing seriously. He deeply mistrusted that flaming red hair.

Chapter Three

"Well, I've done it!" announced Amelia, throwing her hat on the chair and plumping herself down on the sofa next to her aunt, a small, comfortably round woman with a sweet smile and general air of vagueness. She was engaged in embroidering a cushion, and Amelia's abrupt arrival had caused several of the packets of different colored silks to tumble to the well-worn rug.

"What have you done, dearest?" asked her aunt, shuffling her feet in a feeble sort of way, as if she expected the silks to jump back in her lap of their own accord.

"Got a job, aunt," replied her niece, bending down to pick up the little packets. "Secretary to an Earl. Well paid, too, £60 a year, though that's not really the point."

"Isn't it?" replied her aunt vaguely. "Why did you do it then? Though I must say, an extra £60 sounds most welcome to me. Everything is so dreadfully dear these days. It's all because of that scoundrel Bonaparte and them taking all there is for the army. Not that I begrudge it to the poor boys. If anyone needs a good meal, it's those soldiers. But still…." Her voice tailed off, and she picked up her embroidery, her question quite forgotten.

"Oh, aunt, you know we don't need the money. I've explained it all before."

Amelia was very well acquainted with her aunt's inability to concentrate on anything for very long. She had taken her and her twin brother Aurelius in when they were orphaned at the age of fourteen. Never having married, she had had no experience of children before she gave her nephew and niece a home. It had been a trying time for all of them: the twins on the one hand old enough to feel they should be able to fend for themselves, and on the other young enough to still cry privately into their pillows at the memory of their parents.

Theirs had been a happy home. Their mother and father were both descendants of very old families and what remained of what had once been handsome fortunes. Luckily, neither of them was extravagant. Their only real expense, apart from the modest sums they spent on such uninteresting items as food and apparel, was horses. And since they were both fine judges of horseflesh, the animals they invested in for the races and the hunt rarely let them down.

Their other passion was sport of all sorts. It was while in Ireland buying horses that they had seen a game called croquet, and brought it back with them. The neighbors were aghast when the front lawn of their somewhat ramshackle family home was turned into a croquet court, but the whole family enjoyed highly competitive games often lasting far into the summer evenings. The crack of the mallets against the wooden balls and the whoops and hurrahs that followed carried over the fields on the quiet evening air.

When the winter made outdoor exercise impossible, they turned to tennis, which they played on the long upstairs gallery, using small round racquets imported from France before all the troubles began. Over the years, the tennis balls had caused a good deal of damage to the family portraits on the walls and not only to the pieces of china that stood around on small tables, but the tables themselves. When a very old and valuable piece of Sèvres that had been there as long as anyone could remember was smashed beyond repair by a particularly violent return from the lady of the house, everyone agreed it had been hideous and they were better off without it. Anyway, Mama's shot was worth a whole gallery of the ghastly stuff.

They also used the gallery for fencing. Their father began teaching Amelia's brother when he was quite small, but when Amelia ran after them both brandishing her own little wooden sword crying, "me too, me too!" and absolutely refusing to stay out of the way, he gave in and taught them both. Amelia became a fairly good fencer, but Aurelius was far superior. He was naturally a diffident creature and one would never have suspected he harbored a competitive spirit. But his diffidence fell away when he had the épée in his hand, and as he grew taller and more broad-shouldered, Amelia could no longer keep up with him. She would handicap him by making him fence with his left hand, and even then, he was nearly unbeatable. Her temper, never very far from the surface, would cause her to cry hot tears of frustration, but as her mother often told her, it was useless to cry over what one could not change. One should concentrate instead on what one could do something about.

Aurelius was also very keen on boxing, but here both parents absolutely vetoed Amelia's participation. It simply was not done, they said, for a girl to engage in fisticuffs. Not all the temper tantrums in the world could make her mother agree that it was suitable for a young lady to square up to her brother with her fists raised and tell him she was going to plant him a facer. Luckily for him, there were other boys in the neighborhood and then at Eton with whom Aurelius could practice his skill. It was this, moreover, that made him one of the most popular boys of his year, for he was perfectly ready to take on anyone to defend his friends. He would deliver a punishing right with perfect good humor, then help his opponent up and offer him tea and crumpets. It was impossible to dislike him.

But where Amelia excelled was in anything to do with horses. She was accepted as equal to her father as a judge of horseflesh, and compared with her brother was not only the more bruising participant in the hunt, but by far the better whip. She could manage a very spirited pair with an iron wrist and complete imperviousness to the fears of any groom who begged her to "slow down, Miss, for the love of God."

So the happy twins spent the first fourteen years of their lives enthusiastically enjoying one physical activity after the other, paying no attention to the neighbors who declared them unfit for normal society. But it was this attachment to sport that proved the undoing of their parents. Mr. and Mrs. Moreton went on an expedition to Switzerland in the middle of winter to try a sport called snowshoeing. It was described to them as walking with tennis racquets tied to their feet. Unfortunately, they and their whole group of well-to-do British visitors were caught in an avalanche and perished.

The twins, barely recovered from the shock of the death of beloved parents, were told that while their inheritance was certainly enough to live on, they could not expect to stay in the family home. They were too young to live alone. In any case, Aurelius was due to return to Eton at Michaelmas and Amelia could not be left by herself. She argued in vain that she would not be alone. The housekeeper and butler she had known all her life would still be there, and she would have plenty to do. But leaving a fourteen-year-old girl in charge of an estate was simply unacceptable to all the adults who held sway over them.

As she had grown older, Amelia had tried to learn to control her temper, but she lost it on this occasion, and with good reason. It was she who had managed the estate for at least the last two years. She seemed born to take charge, and take charge she did. She had begun by taking over the household accounts from her mother and ended by running her father's affairs as well. To be sure, her father met with the estate agent but it was Amelia who told him what to say and do.

When, in spite of her furious raging, it became clear she could not stay there and the house would have to be rented until Aurelius came of age, Amelia remembered her mother's words. She could do nothing to prevent it, but she could supervise the placement of the advertisements and help interview prospective tenants. In the end, the younger brother of the local squire rented the house and the home farm, and agreed to keep on all the old servants. He was a very amiable man with a young wife and family, and the fact that the place was in some disorder troubled him not at all. In return for very advantageous rental terms, he also agreed to stable the twins' horses and provide them with lodging during the Eton breaks, so they could continue to hunt and ride as before.

The estate agent who would continue to manage the estate until Aurelius came of age was unaware that Amelia had been behind the proposals and decisions of the last couple of years. He smiled condescendingly when he was asked to submit the quarterly accounts to her. However, he subsequently came to value her understanding and sound proposals.

The twins were given a home by aunt Edna, their father's older sister, a pleasant, vague woman who welcomed them both, worried about Aurelius when he went off to Eton and soon left Amelia to take charge. Though her aunt bemoaned the price of household goods that had shot up during the military engagements on the continent, the home had never been run more efficiently or cost effectively. Whereas in the past the housekeeper had allowed stocks to be almost depleted before replacing them, Amelia scoured the newspapers daily, and when she saw a good price for coal or candles, or soap, or oil or starch, or any of the myriad products needed to maintain a household, she bought them. She liked, as she said, to be beforehand with the world.

In the matter of interior furnishings or personal attire, however, Amelia was as uninterested as her mother had been before her. The rug in the salon where aunt Edna was presently embroidering her cushion had definitely seen better days, and Amelia's hat and pelisse were not of this year's, or even last year's vintage. It was true that anyone beholding her was so struck by her vivid red hair and unusual nut-brown eyes that they rarely looked further. Her mouth was a little too wide and her nose a shade too long for classic beauty, especially when she looked down it at individuals who did not have her quick grasp of facts and figures. But she was on the whole held to be a good-looking girl, if a little too managing.

After Aurelius had left Eton, their aunt insisted that they both have dancing lessons. With their natural athleticism, they both excelled at this pastime and enjoyed it. Amelia didn't give a fig what anyone thought of her, and had no ambition to join the fashionable young women of London's society. But they were popular at the low-key parties and balls given by their aunt's friends. Aurelius had his pick of the prettiest girls and Amelia had the gratification of never being a wallflower. Indeed, with her flaming red hair, it would have been impossible for her to pass unnoticed. She even received several offers of marriage. Since these invariably come from dull young men destined to spend their lives in grey offices somewhere in Whitehall, she refused them all as politely as she could, and laughed over them afterwards with her brother.

Amelia was a striking young woman, but her brother was an extremely handsome young man. When they stood together, their likeness was immediately evident, especially about the eyes. But in him the wild bright red hair was replaced by blond curls and if Amelia's countenance lacked classical perfection, his was the embodiment of it. His nose and mouth were exactly right, and his lovely brown eyes shone in a head of classic proportions. That, together with his tall, slim, broad-shouldered physique would have made him the perfect model for one of the statues so recently brought back from Greece by Lord Elgin.

And if his sister was too managing, he was persuadable. At school he found it impossible to say no to any of his friends' proposals. He had been involved in any number of scrapes. His pugilistic ability had often come to his aid, and for the rest, he was saved from more serious punishment than the odd flogging by his ready admission of fault and the disarming smile on his handsome face.

Unlike his sister, he was very interested in his appearance. How could he not be? Every tailor who had ever been honored with his custom had been so pleased to make clothes for a man whose physique was such a thing of perfection, they often professed themselves ready to do it for free. He would be a walking advertisement for their services. He needed no buckram to improve his shoulders nor straw to pad his calves. His arms were not too long, his legs were not too short, his carriage was regal and his neck rose from his shoulders like a column. There was not a style he could not wear and make it look better than the inventor had ever dreamed. From the baggy Petersham trousers to vivid striped pantaloons of the young Tulips, from the high pointed shirt collar with neckcloth up to the chin, to the nipped-in waisted knee-length coat with buttons so large they might have served as saucers, he made it all look wonderful. His tailors sighed as he left them, a vision of perfection every time.

The leavening to this physical excellence was that, for all his prowess, his god-like appearance and unfailing good humor, Aurelius's understanding was not more than moderate. Amelia often commented that the great Roman philosopher whose name he bore must be turning in his grave at some of the idiocies he uttered. Chief amongst them, in her opinion, was his decision not to go to university after leaving Eton. He wanted to go into the army. The Hussars were his preference. He thought them very good fellows and the uniform would become him. Amelia, who would have gone to Oxford like a shot if it had been available to her, would not hear of it.

"No, Aury," she said, in a voice that brooked no disagreement, "the army is not for you. You are so willing to do what anyone tells you, you will get yourself shot within a month. No, you will go to Oxford, to father's old college, and you will become a diplomat. You were born for it. With your looks and address, everyone will love you and no one will notice if you say silly things. You will take the next year to prepare for the entrance exams."

"But Amy," he protested, "You know I ain't bookish. How many of my preps have you done over the years? If you hadn't done those translations of Horace for me I don't know how I could have passed out of Eton. And you hadn't been doing Greek for years, like I had. In fact, I don't think I was ever taught anything else while I was there!"

"No, neither do I. If Papa hadn't insisted on it, I would have taken you out."

"What? And made me leave my friends? Think of the fun I would've missed! Rat races in the Upper Fifth! Conkers in the quad! Cricket matches! Evening parties with the Oppidians!"

"Yes, exactly," said Amelia drily. "It all sounds very educational. But since all the boys from Eton, and no doubt Harrow, did exactly as little as you, you can't be any less prepared than the rest of them."

Aurelius knew it was useless to argue with his sister, but it turned out he was right. Even though she tried to get him ready for entrance to Oxford, when the time came, he failed the exam. She gave him the credit of not believing he had failed deliberately. He was far too honest a man for that. He again tried to convince Amelia that the army was the place for him. But she could point with justice to the fact that with Bonaparte forced to abdicate and exiled on Elba, the army was not in need of new recruits. They would soon be twenty and Amelia realized something had to be done. Her brother was beginning to racket around London with his friends; she knew he needed an occupation to keep him out of trouble.

She was still convinced the diplomatic service was the place for him. He made friends wherever he went, everyone thought well of him and he was, even she had to admit, so very handsome. The foreign dignitaries' wives could not fail to be charmed by him. They would persuade their husbands, and agreements would be reached. Really, he could not fail to be an ornament to any Embassy. Besides, if he were placed in the service of a sensible man, he would not be allowed to get into scrapes. She just had to think of another way of getting him a post.

Not one to be stumped for long, Amelia came up with an idea. She would get a job as a secretary to a man who had the entrée into government, and hence, diplomatic circles. He would be grateful for her excellent work; she would ask him to find a post for her brother and voilà! No sooner was it decided than it was done. She saw the advertisement in The Times. His lordship Edward Woodbridge, Earl of Ailesbury, third Baron of Mayne had no idea what was about to hit him.

Chapter Four

When the Earl arrived home that afternoon, he was looking forward to a bath and dinner before going to the opera. He was not terribly fond of the opera, but he was in the middle of a flirtation with Mrs. Williams, a pretty widow he knew would be there. But he found his secretary Clive Wilson waiting for him in a nervous state.

"Sir," he flustered, "I had the most extraordinary visit from a young lady, a Miss… er Moreton."

"Who?" frowned his lordship. He had entirely forgotten his encounter with that lady earlier in the day.

"Precisely, sir," answered Mr. Wilson. "The more I thought about it, the more it seemed someone had played a… er… practical joke upon your lordship. She arrived with one of your cards with the words 'Hire her' written upon it. I was so dumbfounded, I'm afraid I accepted it and… er, showed her the office, and, I'm very sorry to say, sir, your household accounts." He removed his spectacles and began to polish them furiously.

"Oh! That Miss Moreton! Of course!" His lordship's brow cleared and a twinkle appeared in his eye. "Not to worry, Wilson. I did send her. She's my new secretary."

"But, sir!" expostulated the other man. "She's a woman!"

"Yes, that fact had not escaped my notice. A red-haired woman, as I recall, with nut brown eyes." His lordship's own eyes twinkled even more.

"I didn't notice her eyes, sir, but she did indeed have very red hair." He hesitated. "I fear, sir, she may not be all you desire in a secretary. She appears exceedingly... managing, if I may say."

"She told me she was very organized and prepared to work independently. As you know, I am very disorganized and like nothing more than to be left in peace, so I think she will suit me admirably. Of course, I shall miss you, Wilson, but you may go off in good heart, knowing you have left me in safe hands. In fact, allow me to give you a... er little expression of my esteem."

The Earl went into the office, the poor secretary bumbling behind him. There he wrote him a draft Miss Moreton would have considered excessive for a man who had done no more than his job, and, if all evidence was to be believed, that not very well. Clive Wilson, feeling he had done all he could to warn his volatile employer, thanked the Earl for his generosity, bowed deeply and was gone. He was glad to be leaving a house where he was sure there would soon be trouble. Though he would have liked to be a fly on the wall when Miss Moreton started in with his lordship on the subject of coal.

The Earl proceeded in his leisurely way to bathe, and having donned a pair of close-fitting white pantaloons and a fine cotton shirt topped with a subtle paisley waistcoat, sat in front of his mirror to arrange his neckcloth. His valet held his breath while his lordship took the perfectly ironed foot wide length of muslin and wrapped it swiftly around his collar in a mode known only to himself. He then lowered his chin once or twice onto the folds, looked at it critically and, evidently deeming it acceptable, fixed it in place with an emerald pin. He was helped into a black high-fronted swallow-tailed coat that lay smoothly over his broad shoulders. He took his gold timepiece from the dressing table, put it in his waistcoat pocket with the gold chain looped from a buttonhole, then placed the long ribbon of his quizzing glass around his neck. He drew onto his right hand the heavy signet ring with a curling letter A that had belonged to the head of the family for the last hundred and fifty years, shot his cuffs and, as his valet lightly brushed non-existent particles from his shoulders, took a last look in the mirror before descending the stairs to dinner. If he was not as breathtakingly handsome as Aurelius, he was a very fine figure indeed.

The opera proved to be as unexciting as he had imagined. The soprano had too much vibrato, her generous bosom shaking like a blancmange as she squeezed every ounce of emotion out of the high notes. But the Earl wasn't interested in the soprano's bosom. He quizzed the opulent Mrs. Williams in her box opposite him, received her welcoming smile and during the intermission made his way to her side. The colorless woman who was her ostensible companion obligingly absented herself, and my lord was able to persuade the lady to come to a little *souper à deux* after the show. The outcome of the evening was in every way satisfactory, and both were content when at last they parted. Sybil Williams felt she was a step closer to being a Countess. His lordship was pleased he had been right about the value of the opera and never imagined the lady could have any such notion. If asked, he would have said he supposed he would finally make his choice of a wife amongst the hopeful virgins who crowded the marriage mart every year. But in the meantime, a more experienced partner was just to his taste. The following afternoon he went to Asprey's and had a very fine ruby and diamond bracelet delivered to her. She saw it as a promise of future things; he saw it as thanks for the past.

His lordship's new secretary presented herself at number 23 Albemarle Street at nine thirty the following morning. The Earl was still abed, of course. He rarely appeared before noon except on the days he had appointments at Gentleman Jackson's Boxing Academy. He was a keen amateur boxer and one of the few Mr. Jackson would himself fight a round with. No one ever landed a hit on the champion's person, of course, though the Earl had come close once or twice.

Amelia, however, had no need of her employer, or anyone else. She ensconced herself in the secretary's office and began to open his lordship's letters. She divided them into bills of a personal nature, bills of a household nature, and invitations. She started with the invitations, but these were so numerous and a number of them were to events occurring on the same date, so she quickly realized she would have to ask his lordship which he wanted to accept.

She passed to the personal bills and frowned over what she considered the enormous sums detailed by her employer's tailor, boot and hat makers. She knew from her experience paying Aurelius's bills that gentlemen's clothing was not inexpensive, but these seemed of another order altogether. What she did not know was that the purveyors of these services altered their bills to their customers' circumstances, and since the Earl was known to be rich enough to buy an abbey, as the saying goes, they did not hold back. Aurelius Moreton was a different case altogether. On the one hand, they knew his sister had an eagle eye when it came to bills, and on the other, as we have already seen, they regarded young Moreton as better value than an advertisement in The Times. However, in spite of her misgivings, Amelia did not feel she could engage with her employer on matters of his personal raiment, so though it went against the grain with her to do so, she wrote out the cheques for his signature.

Lastly, she turned to the household bills. She had looked at some of these the day before and had already formed the opinion that his lordship's household was run along profligate lines. The bill from the vintner was astronomical. Surely his lordship alone couldn't drink all that? Deciding to investigate a little, she left the office and penetrated to the fastnesses of the basement kingdom.

She watched Monsieur Antoine, the French chef, in his kitchen for a few moments. He had a junior engaged in making a sauce mousseline to accompany a turbot for his lordship's lunch. The young woman had melted the butter in a small pan, where it was sizzling. Having mixed the egg yolks in a basin, she poured them into the butter. But Amelia could tell the butter was too hot, and sure enough, the result was not a smooth sauce to which cream could be added, but scrambled eggs.

"Idiote!" roared Antoine. "'Ow many times I tell you? Ze butter must not be 'ot! Put eet een ze rubbish and recommence!"

"Pardon, Monsieur," said Amelia, as she watched the girl preparing to scrape the eggs into the rubbish, "but is it necessary to throw away those perfectly good scrambled eggs? I would be glad to eat them for my lunch." Then, as she saw thunder in his face, "The smell of your wonderful cooking has whetted my appetite. With a little bread and butter, and perhaps a piece of cheese, it would be perfect."

It was now close to twelve, and she had breakfasted before eight that morning, so she was ready for lunch. The sous-chef put the eggs on a plate with a slice of bread and a piece of cheese, and placed it on a small table to one side of the kitchen. Amelia sat down with a smile, saying it looked delicious. Unaccustomed to being told anything she did was good, the young woman basked in the thanks before returning to Monsieur Antoine's side. The scullery maid, engaged in scrubbing the pots the chef had used for a few minutes and discarded, goggled at her. Amelia knew it was highly irregular. She should be taking her lunch, not with his lordship, to be sure, but in one of the smaller parlors set aside for such difficult to classify individuals as governesses, seamstresses and now, female secretaries. The whole staff would be discussing it later, but she knew that nothing was better than direct supervision to keep people on their toes.

The mousseline sauce was completed without incident the second time. The turbot was removed from the steamer and placed on a bed of wilted spinach with the sauce in a warm silver sauce boat on the side. It would be served with a dish of souffléd potatoes that came out of the oven, golden and puffy. Nothing could have been more effusive than Miss Moreton's compliments. His lordship was a lucky man, she said to the chef. Not many in London would be enjoying such delicious luncheon, she was sure. The thunder disappeared completely from Monsieur Antoine's face.

She stayed in the kitchen another hour watching the sous-chef assemble the servants' lunch, or dinner, as it would be called. The servants ate their main meal at lunch. Monsieur Antoine's duties were over until his lordship's dinner. He retired to his sitting room with a bottle of wine and what looked like a piece of bread and cheese. It was not uncommon, she knew, for cooks to enjoy very simple meals rather than the complicated dishes they prepared. But she wondered about the wine. If he drank a bottle at lunch every day, and perhaps again at dinner, that would explain the vintner's bill. She would ask the butler. It would usually be he who held the keys to the wine cellar.

The servants' dinner was after his lordship's lunch, when things were quiet in the house. Today they were eating meat pies made of the leftovers of the beef his lordship had had for dinner the night before, put together with gravy and a quantity of root vegetables and served with a pile of boiled potatoes. It would be filling and tasty, but not very fine.

"Monsoor Antoine, he don't like making English food," confided the junior chef. "Pies and that. They don't 'ave 'em over there in France, seemingly. Though 'ow they fills up their bellies with them sauces and the like, I'm sure I don't know."

Amelia forbore to respond that from all she had heard, many of the French people didn't fill up their bellies with anything. That was one of the reasons they'd got rid of their king. Whether things were better now, she didn't know. Bonaparte had apparently escaped from Elba and the country was in uproar again. Many who had appeared to welcome the monarchy when it returned after Boney's abdication were now rising up and marching with him again. She just hoped she could keep her brother from marching against him.

Chapter Five

When she calculated that the Earl would have finished his lunch, she made her way upstairs, and having collected the sheaf of invitations and the unsigned cheques from the office, tapped at the dining room door. She discovered him leaning back in his chair sipping from a glass of wine and smoking a cigar. He was thinking about the night before and deciding to go to Asprey's. Bullock had cleared the remains of lunch and had gone to eat his own meal. The Earl gave a start as she entered and stood up, putting down both his glass and the cigar.

"Miss... er...," he appeared to be searching for her name.

"Moreton. Amelia Moreton," she said helpfully. "Please sit down and continue with your wine and cigar. What we have to do won't take too long."

He eyed the bunch of papers in her hand. "I hope not, Miss Moreton," he said depressingly. "You will find I dislike business as much as you apparently enjoy it. Please sit down. You must know I cannot do so unless you do."

"It will be much easier if you cease to think of me as a female, sir," said Amelia. "I am simply your secretary. Treat me as you treated Mr. Wilson."

His lordship thought that if Claud Wilson had come into the dining room with a sheaf of papers when he was enjoying a post-prandial cigar, he would have told him to go to the devil. But then, Claud Wilson hadn't had that mass of red hair, that white skin and those brown eyes. Like most people, the Earl's survey of Amelia had stopped there, and he was barely aware of her rather outmoded gown in a dark brown, the decorously high neckline enlivened only by a narrow white collar. He moved to pull out a chair for her, and she sat down.

"May I offer you a glass of wine, Miss Moreton?" asked his lordship, though as he looked around, he realized there were no other glasses on the table.

"No thank you, sir," she responded, to his relief, "but please feel free to continue the enjoyment of yours, and your cigar. My father used to enjoy one after meals and the aroma has never disturbed me. As I said, this won't take long. First, I must ask you to sign these cheques."

To his astonishment, she pulled from her hair what he had taken to be a brown hairpin of vaguely Japanese appearance, but which turned out to be a pen with a well-mended nib, and from a pocket on the side of her gown she drew a bottle of ink. She handed them both to her employer, together with the first of the cheques. She was prepared to explain what each bill had been for, but he didn't read either the payee or the amount, but simply signed it with the one word: Ailesbury. She handed him the other cheques one by one and he did the same with them all.

"Well," she said with a slight laugh, "I could have signed them myself had I realized you have no interest in knowing who you're giving money to and why."

"Yes, why didn't you?" he answered unconcernedly, finishing the last one. "I feel sure that if there had been a problem you wouldn't have given it to me to sign. My signature is quite easy to copy."

A little incensed by his cavalier attitude, she retorted, "Oh, I don't say I have no problem with the bills, but I thought your lordship would dislike my discussing it. The one for boots from Hoby, for example, is nearly twice what he charged my brother for essentially the same thing: gold tasseled Hessians. They are no doubt very fine, but the price you paid is exorbitant."

"Indeed?" commented his lordship, raising a brow. "Though we could look at it the other way round. Perhaps what he charged me was the normal price and what he charged your brother was a significant reduction. Since I don't know your brother, I cannot say why that should be."

Thinking of her god-like brother and her own discussions with Hoby on the matter of suitable boots for a young man on his way to Oxford, Amelia was inclined to think perhaps her employer was right.

"Hmm," she said. "There is some justice in what you say."

His lordship's eyes twinkled with amusement. "Thank you," he responded seriously, with a slight bow of his head.

"He is so amazingly handsome, that's the thing," she confided. "He's my twin, but we don't look a bit alike." In this she was, of course, mistaken, but his lordship had no way of knowing it.

"No red hair?" he suggested.

"No, he's very fair and looks like a Greek statue. It really is most problematic. Everyone is immediately drawn to him, as one always is to things of beauty. And he is so pleasant, everyone likes him and will give him just about anything. I can't tell you the number of scrapes I've had to extricate him from, especially with young women, who all fall in love with him."

"Lucky fellow," murmured the Earl.

"No, it isn't," said Amelia, before thinking. "I need to establish him creditably and...." Then she collected herself. "But we're not here to talk about Aurelius."

"Aurelius? That's a very grand name," commented her employer.

"Yes, isn't it? Though, because he looks like a statue, it suits him. Except that...," she tailed off. She had been going to say except he's not always very sensible, but since she was hoping to find her brother a job through the Earl's contacts, it would not do for him to think him unintelligent.

His lordship looked enquiringly at her, "Except that...?"

"Except it doesn't give a good idea of what he's really like," she ended. Quickly, before her employer could ask any more questions about her family, she went on, "Now we need to deal with the matter of your invitations. You have so many, and some for the same day. To which should I answer yes, and to which no?"

The Earl sighed and held out his hand. Amelia passed the pile to him.

"No, no, no, no, yes, yes, perhaps, no, no, yes, yes, yes, no," he said, tossing them back one by one.

"Wait!" she exclaimed. "I have to make sure I've got it. The first four were no." She put a small n at the top of each. "Then these two are yes's, this is a perhaps," she marked them y, y and p respectively. "I shall ask you about the perhaps in a day or two. Then we had two no's, three yes's and a no." She marked the rest.

"You are remarkably quick, Miss Moreton," said her employer, admiringly. "As a hint, let me tell you I never go to a musical evening other than the opera, which I sometimes appreciate." He thought about Sybil Williams and smiled to himself. "The caterwauling gives me a headache. Or, at least, I pretend it does. I do, however, usually go to balls; I like to dance and if there are no partners to tempt me I can always play cards. Outdoor entertainments such as ridottos, *al fresco* parties and the like I don't mind if the company is good. You'll soon find out which I think good and which I don't. If they are hosted by the younger set, they're usually worth going to, if it's older hostesses they're generally a dead bore, with all the matrons sitting around commenting that they never did things like that when they were young. Tea parties are an absolute no. I positively dislike tea and I've never learned the trick of holding a saucer in one hand, a cake in the other, and still being able to pick up the cup. I'm convinced it is a feminine attribute. For dinners, you had better let me see who the invitation is from until you get to know my circle better. Sometimes they can be quite pleasant but I have no desire to be caught sitting next to one of the matrons I just referred to. In a week or two I daresay you will know me well enough to answer the invitations for me."

What he did not say was that should there be a lady who had caught his eye and he knew she was going to be at any of those events, he would go no matter what. But he was known for being volatile and could always change his mind at the last minute. He was charming, he was handsome and he was rich. No hostess would ever refuse to accommodate him.

"I hope I'm able to save you as much trouble as possible, my lord," said Amelia demurely.

As she left the dining room, she thought that his lordship gave every indication of being very spoiled and would be the better for a set-down or two. But she would have to guard herself against that. She was there to make herself indispensable.

She spent the afternoon penning acceptances to the invitations her employer had accepted and polite refusals to those he had not. On the whole, she was inclined to approve his choices. Tea parties and musical evenings had never interested her either. A good gallop or a horse race were much more to her taste. She left the pile of envelopes with the butler, asking him to have them delivered as soon as may be.

"We'll do the best we can, Miss, but there's always such a number young Wilkins can't always get to them all without ignoring some of his other duties. He may have to deliver some of them tomorrow."

"That will be satisfactory, I'm sure," she replied, putting on her pelisse and uncompromising bonnet and leaving the house.

When she got home. Aurelius was all agog with the news from Europe. Bonaparte had landed near Cannes with a thousand men and, to avoid royalist Provence, had taken a route over the Alps.

"Just imagine, Amy," said her brother. "He stood in front of his men outside Grenoble and opened his coat to the royalist army, saying if any of you will shoot his Emperor, here I am. Instead of shooting at him, they all joined with him and now he's on his way to Paris! He may be a scoundrel, but by God, he has courage!"

"I daresay, but I hear he has grown quite corpulent and has trouble staying on his horse for long."

Their heated discussion carried on all through dinner, with their poor aunt looking from one to the other in bewilderment.

"Why, Aury!" she exclaimed at one point, "One would almost think you are a supporter of Bonaparte! I cannot imagine why. It's all his fault the price of oil has doubled!"

"No, aunt," laughed her nephew. "I'm not a supporter! God knows, he belongs back in exile, but you have to admire his style!"

Soon after dinner, however, Aurelius took his leave of the ladies, saying he was going out with a couple of excellent chaps who knew some good places where a fellow could kick up his heels.

"I hope he doesn't get into trouble," sighed Amelia. "But what can I do? He has his own income and he isn't a child. But now he's not going to Oxford, I must find him something useful to do. The quicker I can win the Earl's confidence, the better."

Chapter Six

The next morning, Amelia was surprised to see the Earl leaving the house just as she had come in.

"My goodness," she said, "you are up betimes, my lord! I thought you were never abroad before lunch."

"By no means, Miss Moreton," he answered. "You are not the only early bird around here. I frequently see the morning sun, though not," he admitted with a boyish grin, "as often as I see it setting."

It was impossible not to be caught by his good humor. "Then since today is one of your early days," she answered, "perhaps you will be so kind as to see me when you return? I'm sure I shall have questions for you. Shall you be back before lunch?"

His face fell, ludicrously. "Is this the reward I am to receive for my virtuous behavior?" he cried. "Absolve me, Miss Moreton, from having to both rise early and do business before lunch. Didn't you say yesterday you wished to save me from as much trouble as possible? Then sign my name to cheques, if you please, accept or deny invitations on my behalf, and please, I beg you, don't ruin my digestion by asking me questions at lunch. Monsieur Antoine is an artist in the kitchen, but it will quite ruin my enjoyment of what he prepares for me if I know I am to receive a solemn-faced person with pile of papers and a pen after my meal."

Amelia laughed. "Was I solemn-faced? I didn't mean to be! But I was talking about seeing you before lunch, not during or after. Do you think you could manage that? If I may just have a few more minutes of your time, I'm sure that thereafter you need see me hardly ever again."

"Miss Moreton," he replied solemnly, "I hope I am not so lacking in manners as to imply I never wish to see you again. It's the papers and the pen I don't want to see, even if the pen is doubling as a hairpin."

She blushed. "Did I do that? Oh, yes, I did, I remember now. My brother laughs at me, but, you know, it's a very convenient way of always having a pen about one."

His eyes twinkled. "I imagine it is. Now, Miss Moreton, I must be off. If I keep him waiting, Gentleman Jackson will doubtless find a way of making me pay."

"Oh! Do you box with him?" cried Amelia. "Aurelius is always saying he wishes he could have seen him fight Mendoza, but, of course, that was before we were born. He will be quite eaten with jealousy when I tell him."

"Ah yes, the Greek statue. Does he enjoy the sport?"

"Yes. I'm told he's very good, but, of course, I have never seen it, I'm glad to say." She shuddered. "He often talks about the science of it. It's funny, although we both very much enjoy most sports, that is one I cannot abide."

"I believe few women do," answered his lordship, quite seriously. "Well, you must bring Aurelius here one morning and I'll take him with me. I go on Tuesdays and Thursdays most weeks. Bring him next Tuesday, why don't you?"

He was gone before Amelia could express her thanks. She was delighted. Here was the introduction she had hoped for! If the Earl liked Aury, he would certainly help him. For his part, her employer was amused at the opportunity of meeting this young god. There were obviously things Miss Moreton had not said and he looked forward to finding out what they were.

With her employer out of the house, Amelia decided it was a good moment to talk to Mr. Bullock about the wine stores. She found him in his sitting room, checking the silver. She introduced the matter obliquely, first by asking him how long he'd been with the Earl.

"Oh, Miss," he said. "I was taken on when I was just 16 as an under-footman by the late Earl, his lordship's father. He had just married her ladyship and was setting up his own establishment. He wasn't Earl then, of course. His father, the present Earl's grandfather, was still alive and living here. Then, when he passed away I came here with the new Earl, and gradually worked my way up. I remember the present Earl being born. He has an older sister, but she's been with her husband in Vienna these last two years."

"Is he a diplomat? The Earl's sister's husband, I mean," said Amelia, trying not to sound too excited. This was perfect! All her employer had to do was recommend Aury to his brother-in-law!

"Yes, Miss, sent there by the Regent himself."

"That's perfect!" said Amelia, before she could stop herself. Then, realizing what she had said, added, "I mean, diplomacy is a perfect profession for a gentleman. Anyway," she hurried on, "it must be a great solace to his lordship to have such a long-time employee with him to run things."

"I hope to give satisfaction, Miss," said the old man gravely. "His lordship is a most undemanding employer, I have to say."

"Yes, he leaves a lot to you, I expect." She hesitated. "Ordering the wine, for instance."

Bullock looked at her for a moment but said nothing. Amelia decided to be blunt.

"Look, Mr. Bullock, I've been dealing with the bills. The one for the wine seems very high for a bachelor. Then yesterday, I noticed that Monsieur Antoine took a bottle with him for lunch. I thought that if he did that for lunch and dinner every day, that would account for it. You hold the keys to the wine cellar, don't you? You must know."

The old man was silent and then said a little defensively, "Mr. Wilson never mentioned anything about it, and I'm surprised you picked up on it so quickly. The fact is, Moosure Antoine came to me when he was first engaged, oh, three years ago it was, and said he was accustomed to cooking with wine, and would I give him a key to the wine cellar. That way he could get a bottle out when he needed it. I told him to tell me what he wanted and I'd get it. But he said that would be impossible because he might need three different bottles for different things and he couldn't be always thinking about it in advance. He was an artist, he said. Got quite agitated, he did. You know what these frogs are like! So not wanting to cause a fuss, I let him have the second key. There's only two. His late lordship used to keep the other one, but when he died it was put in the desk in here. I offered it to his present lordship, but he just laughed the way he does, and told me just to make sure there was always enough in the cellars for him. He told me to order what we need when we need it, and that's what I've done."

He was quiet for a moment, then went on, a little reluctantly, "Of course, I realized quite quickly Moosure was doing more than cooking with the wine. He was drinking it like a fish. I did speak to him about it, but he got agitated again and said he'd go to his lordship, or just leave. There's plenty of others who'd have him, he said. And you know, the Earl does enjoy his cooking. He's always talking about it and saying he eats better at home than anywhere, so I just let it go." The butler looked down at his desk and sighed.

"Is it getting worse, do you think?" asked Amelia.

"No, it's about the same as it's ever been."

"Well, then, let's just keep an eye on it. I'll tell Monsieur Antoine I know what he's doing, but I won't say anything to his lordship… yet. You're right. His lordship does enjoy the cooking. He was telling me so just today."

"Thank you, Miss. To tell you the truth, I'm glad there's someone else that knows. It's been exercising me a bit, I can tell you."

Amelia stood up. She held out her hand to the old man. "Have no fear, Mr. Bullock. I'm on your side!"

He stood up and shook her hand.

Next, the indefatigable Amelia went to see the housekeeper. She found her, too in her sitting room, looking at a book containing the lists of the household linens. She explained that she had been doing the accounts and found the household consumption of candles and coal very high for a bachelor establishment. Mrs. Hancock, at first inclined to take exception to the comment, soon became more amenable when Amelia explained that she'd been keeping house herself one way and the other ever since she was a girl. She knew how hard it was keeping everything straight. The housekeeper explained that the candle consumption was due to the fact that the servants replaced all the candles with new every day. That had been the practice ever since she'd been there, which was about seven years.

"I believe it was on the orders of her ladyship before she moved to Deering in the country, and it has just been kept up," she said.

"Has his lordship ever been asked whether he prefers new candles every day?" asked Amelia.

It seemed that his lordship had not. "And what happens to the burnt-down candles," she continued, "surely they are not simply put in the rubbish? A good beeswax candle will last three or four days."

"Well, of course, we use them in the servants' quarters and… and…." Mrs. Hancock became a little reticent. "Well, the truth is, Miss, we sell the rest and put the money into a kitty for Christmas time. That way, they all get a little bonus for the holidays."

"I see, and who distributes this bonus?"

"I take care of the female staff and Mr. Bullock takes care of the men."

"And yourselves, too, I take it?"

Mrs. Hancock had the grace to blush. "Yes, ourselves too," she admitted.

"And is it clear this bonus comes from his lordship's pocket, or does the staff think you and Mr. Bullock are distributing largesse?"

"Well, I couldn't rightly say. We've never really explained…."

"I see." Amelia did see. It was very pleasant to be thought the source of the bonuses and they no doubt encouraged personal loyalty. "Coming to the coal consumption," she said. "What is the story there?"

Mrs. Hancock explained that this, too was a legacy from her ladyship. As she got older, she felt the cold, as one does, and required that fires be lit in all the rooms, even when they were not being used. She had the idea that a cold room drew the heat from a warm one. The practice had simply carried on.

"How many bedrooms are there, apart from his lordship's?" asked Amelia. She had not been to any part of the house beyond the ground floor. She had been aware, however, that it was remarkably warm in the house.

"Nine, Miss, not counting the servants' quarters. But there are no fires up there. And there's the ballroom, of course."

"There's a ballroom?"

"Yes, on the first floor. There are four fireplaces in there, but we do only light two." The housekeeper seemed proud of their restraint.

"So you are lighting twelve fireplaces upstairs every day, plus how many downstairs?"

"Well, there's the big one in the salon, two in the dining room, one in the billiard room, one in your office, Miss, one in the library, one in the blue parlor and one in her ladyship's parlor."

"And who uses her ladyship's parlor?"

"No one, Miss. Except when her ladyship comes. She uses it."

"And how often does she come?"

"Perhaps a month a year in the season."

"So, twelve fireplaces upstairs, eight downstairs and how many down here in the servants' quarters?"

"Well, there's my sitting room, Mr. Bullock's sitting room, Moosure Antoine's, and the kitchen. Four, but the kitchen fireplace is very big. It used to be used for cooking, but not these days."

"Altogether, then, twenty-four fireplaces all burning merrily all day long from, say, October till May?" concluded Amelia, then added, "For a bachelor living alone."

"When you put it like that, Miss, it does sound a lot," agreed Mrs. Hancock unhappily.

"However you put it," said Amelia tartly, "it sounds like a lot. But have no fear, this is not of your making. I'll talk to his lordship. Perhaps he agrees with his mother. We'll see."

Chapter Seven

Unaware that decisions of a housekeeping nature were to be laid before him, the Earl returned home later that morning. He had had a vigorous round with Gentleman Jackson, narrowly avoiding a hit from the famous left jab. Refreshed by a hosing down from a cold pipe, he was now very hungry and looking forward to his lunch. He wondered what Monsieur Antoine would have prepared for him today.

As soon as he stepped into the hall and handed his hat and cane to Bullock, Miss Moreton appeared. She had been keeping an eye out for him.

"Fifteen minutes of your time, sir," she said, and, not waiting for an answer, turned back towards her office. When her employer did not appear to be following her, she stopped, looked back and said, "The sooner we have this little talk, the sooner I shall leave you to your lunch."

She spoke not unlike someone admonishing a recalcitrant four-year-old, and the Earl did, in fact, suddenly have a clear memory of his old nanny using just such a tone. He sighed and followed her.

Amelia sat behind her desk and gestured to the seat in front of it. Now her employer felt like a boy called before the beak at Eton and wondered suddenly what he had done wrong. It soon became clear. He had entirely failed to keep the reins of his household firmly in his grasp. He had allowed the profligate use of candles and coal.

"If you wish these practices to continue, sir, we need say no more," his secretary was concluding, "but," as she saw him beginning to nod and rise to his feet, "I think there is perhaps a better way."

Reluctantly, he sat down again. "And I'm sure, Miss Moreton, you're going to tell me what it is," he said.

"Yes. I propose you direct the housekeeper to use new candles every day in the public rooms. I agree with her ladyship that half-used candles give the wrong impression. But in the other rooms, they are to be used up as much as is reasonable. Then, in place of the Christmas bonus the sale of used candles provided, I suggest you give your servants a seasonal gratuity of ten percent of their wages. This is something that is easily accounted for in the books and will probably be covered by the reduction in outgoing for candles. In this way, your servants will know who is responsible for this generosity and their allegiance to you will be enhanced."

His lordship had never doubted his servants' allegiance, for he was a kind and generous master. But everyone except perhaps Mr. Bullock and Mrs. Hancock, who would not have been human if they had not kept a disproportionate portion of bonus for themselves, was delighted with the new régime when the time came. A ten percent gratuity was more than they had ever been given.

"As for the coal, I propose that the fires be lit twice a week only in the unused rooms. Again, I agree with her ladyship that they should not be left to get cold and damp. The work saved will be advantageous too, for the maids will have more time to attend to other duties. I daresay the books in the library need dusting, and... other things."

Since Amelia had never done anything of the sort in her life, she gave no details of what those other things might be. But she knew this would save money and said so.

"But, my dear Miss Moreton," said his lordship, when he heard this. "You begin to trouble me. Am I so much in queer street that I need to save money on coal? I had no idea. Wilson never mentioned it. How fortunate I engaged you when I did!" His eyes twinkled in a way she had begun to recognize.

"Of course not! You know that isn't the case. Your lordship is as rich as... as...."

"Croesus?" suggested his lordship. "If that is still so, I'm glad. I don't think I'd like being poor."

"You may be as rich as you like," replied Amelia sternly, "but it is never a good idea to simply throw money away. If you have money to burn, quite literally, there are charitable institutions I can suggest."

"Please do, Miss Moreton. I'm sure any charity you suggest would be admirable. In fact, all your suggestions are admirable and I heartily agree to them. Now, please may I have my lunch. I really am quite hungry. May I ask you to join me?" he added on an impulse.

"No. That is, no thank you, I shall take my lunch in the kitchen. I like to see what's going on down there. And no, you may not have your lunch until you've told me how you want me to answer these other letters." She spread them before him. "This is from...."

But he cut her off. He stood up. "I'm sorry, but I must say no to you, Miss Moreton, I've told you before. Answer them any way you choose. Just tell me afterwards where I am engaged, when and to whom. You may tell them all to go to the devil for all I care. Now I am going to have my lunch." He strode out of the room. Amelia looked after him, shaking her head. Men, she thought. When her brother was hungry there was no speaking to him about anything but his dinner. It seemed his lordship was exactly the same.

The following Tuesday, Aurelius came to Albemarle Street with his sister, for once willing to rouse himself at what he considered an ungodly hour of the morning. At home in the country he had been accustomed to exercising the horses and was rarely a late riser. But here, having no horses and, indeed, no real occupation, he had taken to frolicking into the early hours at unsavory haunts in very undesirable parts of town. It was as well his sister knew nothing about this, nor how, under the influence of cheap gin, he had taken to risking considerable amounts of money on ridiculous wagers such as which cockroach would drown first in a mug of beer. These were the sorts of activities he had been in trouble for at Eton, but there the beaks had kept it under control. Now there was no restraint at all.

But this morning, knowing he was to meet the Earl, he had been up betimes and had taken particular care with his appearance. He was looking extremely fine. His lordship's eyes twinkled characteristically as he beheld the young Apollo, and considered his secretary had told him nothing less than the truth about her brother. He did, however, think her wrong in saying there was no resemblance between them. Her nose and wide mouth kept her from his classical beauty, but the eyes and tilt of the head were the same. And now that he looked at her for the first time from the neck down, he saw that under her unimpressive gown, her figure was as magnificent as his. She could have modelled for the prow of a ship. Seen together, they were an arresting pair.

At the pugilist's Academy, Aurelius was gratified to be brought to the attention of Gentleman Jackson himself. When he had stripped and fought a few rounds with one of the many acolytes who always hung around the rings, the champion was able to give him a few hints on his science. The body was to be held with the head and shoulders in a slight forward bend, the hands well up in a defensive position, fists alone were to be used; there was to be no kicking or mauling.

Privately he told the Earl, "Good lad. Not often abroad in his punches. He'll do well, very well, if he can watch the other man close, learn his weakness. Let him come in and watch, fight a few rounds like today. Friend of yours, sir?"

"Not exactly. Friend of a friend, you might say," replied his lordship. "I'd be grateful if you'd keep an eye on him."

"Will do, sir. He shows promise, no doubt about that."

Aurelius was overjoyed when he heard what Gentleman Jackson had said, and shook the Earl's hand in a grip like a vise, his brown eyes shining like polished chestnuts. Then when he was invited to White's for lunch, his cup was full. He had heard of the famous club, of course, but as it was the preserve of the Tory aristocracy, he had never entered its hallowed portals. That evening, when he told Amelia about his triumph (as he saw it) at Gentleman Jackson's, and his pleasure at being introduced to his lordship's cronies, his enthusiasm made him seem more boyish than ever.

"They're all a bit older, of course, but very good chaps," he said, smiling from ear to ear, "very civil. I tell you, Amy, it was something like!"

Amelia, for her part, was delighted that her plan was progressing. She did not expect her employer to befriend her brother exactly, but to be aware of him, to see him from time to time and to know they had something in common, apart from herself. That was enough at this stage.

"If you take him as your model rather than some of the nincompoops I've seen in your company recently, it will be no bad thing," she said. "Though he doesn't seem to take things very seriously, he is most surely a gentleman."

The Earl, not knowing he was being groomed to perform an important role in the young man's future, thought him a very pleasant fellow. When he saw him at Gentleman Jackson's over the next few weeks, he always stopped for a word and followed his progress.

Amelia did as she had been instructed and answered the notes and letters to her employer as she saw fit. If an entertainment appealed to her, she accepted. His lordship was thus engaged to watch the launch of a hot air balloon, accompany a party to see a tattoo performed by the Royal Horse Guards at the Vauxhall Gardens, where they were to play the silver kettledrums presented to them by the king himself ten years before, and enjoy an *al fresco* luncheon at Hampton Court. She was not to know until she informed her employer of one of these engagements a few days before it was to occur, that she had erred.

"Good God! Why am I to watch a hot air balloon in the company of that whey-faced daughter of the Harringtons?" he asked her in astonishment, coming in to her office one afternoon, waving the invitation and the reminder. "You surely did not accept?"

"I thought a hot air balloon launch might be interesting," she explained.

"And so it might, were it not for the simpering miss they're bound to thrust at me!" He turned the missive over. "It's the day after tomorrow! Too late for me to cry off! Miss Moreton, what have I done that you should want to punish me so?"

"Nothing," she laughed. "It's your own fault. You told me to answer how I liked, and I did!"

"I didn't mean how you liked but how you thought I liked."

"But how am I supposed to know which invitations include whey-faced daughters and which do not?" she asked, not unreasonably. "If I asked you, you'd tell me to go to the devil!"

"I most certainly would not," retorted his lordship. "I have never spoken to a woman like that in my life."

"We are agreed that I'm not a woman, I'm your secretary. I know you often wish to tell me to go to the devil, so you might as well do it. I don't mind. Anyway, the balloon will be fun. You can croak a few words and tell her you have laryngitis. Say you're fascinated by the ascent. Then you won't have to talk to her."

He laughed. "Is that what you would do?"

"No," she said, "I'd just tell him I found him a total bore and to please go way. But you can't do that. You're a gentleman. I'm not."

"You're not a gentleman and you're not a woman. What are you Miss Moreton?"

"I'm your secretary who has a lot to do, so please go away. Though," she conceded, "you're not a total bore."

He bowed and went to the door saying, "I'm relieved to hear it. I feel sure you would tell me if I were."

But a worse blunder was to come.

Chapter Eight

From time to time, the Earl received missives on perfumed paper from ladies he had danced with or accompanied into dinner the night before, expressing their delight at having made his acquaintance. Amelia judged, rightly, that they were not innocent girls, who would never have written to gentleman on so slight a connection. The first time, she placed one before him without comment, but he flicked it away with a fastidious finger saying, "I generally respond to these with one of my cards simply saying Lord Ailesbury thanks Miss so and so for her note and presents his compliments. I find that depresses any pretentions."

"If I received a response like that," she commented. "I'd be absolutely furious!"

He smiled at her. "I'm sure you would, and you would probably march right round to give me a set-down. But, Miss Moreton, I'm convinced you would not have written such a note to me in the first place, so the situation would never arise."

She had to agree he was right. The idea of writing to a bachelor gentleman on any pretext other than business was repugnant to her. A week or so later, her employer received a note written on a paper in a violent shade of pink, with a pungent aroma of ambergris, a scent that she particularly disliked.

Dear Ned, (it read)
or should I say my lord though now we are
partickular freinds I feel Ned is better, I am writing
because I have seen the deerest ear-rings in Asprey's
ekzacly like the bracelet you gave me I think it must
be a set and I know you will want to get them for me
before they are gone.
Your Sybil

Amelia was utterly astonished. First, it had never occurred to her that the Earl could go by the name of Ned. She knew his name was Edward, but Ned! It was the name she and her brother had given the rocking horse in their nursery! She was not to know he had been called that from birth to avoid confusion with his father who bore the same name. Secondly, she was shocked he had given a gift to a woman who barely knew how to write or spell! And it was entirely outside her experience that any woman could be so lost to propriety that she would ask a man not a close relative to buy her something. There must be some mistake. She hesitated, but deciding she should simply follow his lordship's directions, she drew out one of his cards and wrote in a fine clear hand:

Lord Ailesbury thanks you for your
communication but regrets he cannot do as you
wish.

She hesitated again, wondering if she had done the right thing. But her employer had told her unequivocally to answer things as she saw fit, so she picked up an envelope, addressed it and put it with the others for delivery.

The result of this was that when the Earl saw Sybil Williams at a rout a few days later, she turned a pouting face upon him.

Surprised, since they had last parted on the best of terms, he asked what the matter was.

"How can you ask, Ned?" she said reproachfully. "After what you wrote me."

"I? Wrote to you? You must be mistaken, my dear. And if I had, I would not have said anything to deserve your reproach." He smiled winningly.

"For sure, I know gentlemen sometimes do things in their cups they don't remember afterwards." she said, removing a folded card from her tiny reticule, "I made sure you must have been a little... shall we say, not quite yourself when you wrote this." She thrust the card at him.

He took it and unfolded it, recognizing it as one of his own. When he saw the message and the handwriting, he had to swallow the laugh that came unbidden to his lips.

"I see. Of course, there has been some mistake. And what was it you wished me to do? My... er memory is so bad."

"Oh, Ned, I knew you couldn't be so mean! It was the matching pair of earrings I saw in Asprey's last week!"

"You mean matching...."

"The darling bracelet. I knew you would want me to have the set. I think they are still there." She knew they were, for she had checked only that morning, knowing she was going to see the Earl at the rout.

"Then I shall move heaven and earth to make them yours tomorrow, dear Sybil," replied Ned.

The rest of the evening and part of the night passed exactly as each had planned. The Earl had got what he wanted and Sybil thought she had too. However, far from diverting the planets from their course, his lordship simply sent a footman to Asprey's the next morning with a note and a card to be delivered with the earrings. Sybil Williams would have been less pleased with herself had she known the card she would receive from his lordship this time would gently but firmly put an end to their relationship. He did not like getting demanding letters from his inamorata and, for some reason he could not fully articulate, he liked even less that his secretary knew about it.

When Amelia opened the bill from Asprey's a few days later, she remembered the note she had written. Apparently, the earrings had been purchased after all, and for a sum that made her blink. Instead of signing the cheque on behalf of her employer, as she was now doing with the regular bills, she took it with her when she went to speak to the Earl on another matter. Their meetings had become infrequent since she had taken over almost completely and it was several days before she saw him.

"I did not like to sign a cheque of this magnitude for you," she said, placing the bill before him. "In case it was a mistake."

"You know very well it is not a mistake, Miss Moreton," replied his lordship, twinkling at her. "For you tried to save me the expense, as I recall. But," he said, scrawling his name on the cheque, "I think it made a very nice parting gift, don't you?"

Unusually, Amelia could find nothing to say.

Chapter Nine

The following morning as she walked smartly up Albemarle Street towards number 23, Amelia noticed a ragged urchin sitting against the railings of the dark steps that led down to the kitchens of one of the townhouses. It was an early spring morning, and she was glad of her coat. The boy was hardly clothed enough for midsummer. His filthy and almost skeletal bare arms were trembling with cold. She stopped.

"What are you doing there, child?" she asked kindly.

"Please, Miss," he said "can yer spare a few coppers fer a slice o' bread? I ain't et nuffin since yesterday."

Amelia opened her reticule and handed the boy some pennies. He grabbed them and made off before she had a chance to ask him how he came to be there. Beggars were common enough in the East End, she knew, but here in Mayfair they were rare. The Watch moved them along.

The next day as she was once again walking towards her place of employment, she was accosted by the same boy. He was once again crouched against the railings leading down to the basement of one of the houses and she didn't see him until he caught at her skirt. In fact, she realized, it was a good place to hide. It was naturally dark down there and his skin and clothes were of such almost uniform blackness, he was practically invisible.

"Please, Miss, I don't mean no 'arm," he said. "Only I arsked them inside down there for a bit o' sumpfin to eat, but they told me to get lorst. Then I sees you an' you was nice to me yesterday."

"But where is your home?" she asked. "Where do you live? You can't continue to stay on the steps along here."

"I ain't got no 'ome, Miss. I was workin' in the fact'ry where me Pa left me when me Ma died, but they is so 'ard there. Old Skillins, 'e beats yer if yer stops for a minute. And I's allers so 'ungry. So I run away. Came up 'ere to the West End. I 'eard there's people 'ere wiv money and they gives yer food. But I ain't found a one as does. Ceptin' you."

"Well," said Amelia, "you can't stay here. You'd better come with me. What's your name?"

"Tom, Miss."

"Tom what? What is your surname?"

"I don't know, Miss."

"How old are you?"

"I don't rightly know that neither, Miss. Me dad left me ever so long ago."

She looked at him. He was pitifully thin and could have been any age from ten to fourteen. She hesitated to take the boy's filthy hand, but then chided herself for her lack of Christian feeling and took it. There were only a few steps to go, luckily, and they were at number 23. She told Tom to go down to the basement entrance and she would be with him in a few minutes. She did not want to have to deal with Bullock's inevitable protests. Having removed her coat and hat, she went immediately down into the kitchen and through to the scullery where the door to the basement was located. She opened it and drew the reluctant boy in.

The scullery maid took one look at him and shrieked, "Lawks, Miss! What you doin' with that dirty boy in 'ere? He's probly infested with vermin! Whatever will Mrs. 'Ancock say?"

"That is my problem, not yours. Bring a basin of warm water and soap over here for Tom to wash his face and hands, while I find him something to eat. Then you get on with your work."

"I don't need to wash me 'ands and face, Miss," protested Tom. "You just give me a bit of summat and I'll scarper."

"You will do no such thing," replied Miss Moreton. "You cannot continue to live on the street and until I have had a few words with your master, I will not have you return to your place of work. Do as I say. Wash your face and hands."

Amelia went into the kitchen and spoke to the young sous-chef, whose name she had learned was Annie, she of the scrambled eggs. She disappeared and in a couple of minutes reappeared with a large piece of bread, two slices of ham and a mug of milk. When these delights were placed in front of young Tom, he could hardly believe his eyes. Looking furtively to left and right, he began to gobble it down, his unused hand and arm curled around the plate, as if he feared it would be taken away at any second.

"Slowly, Tom, slowly!" said Amelia. There is no rush. I'm going to speak to Mrs. Hancock to see what can be done with you. Stay here like a good boy and don't run away. I'll give you some bread and jam when I get back."

If the thought of running away once he had eaten what was on his plate had crossed Tom's mind, the promise of bread and jam was irresistible. He had heard about it, but never in his life tasted it. He stayed put.

Amelia knocked on the housekeeper's door and went in. Their relationship was now one of mutual respect. The modifications made to the consumption of coal had made Mrs. Hancock life easier. The maids were less occupied making up fires and could do other housework, including the darning and ironing. The housekeeper consequently had less of a sense that she was always behind. So when Amelia explained what had happened and asked for help getting Tom cleaned up and clothed, in spite of her misgivings, she agreed.

"Once he is fed and presentable, I shall take him back to this factory and see what the terms of his employment are," said Miss Moreton. "I have the feeling he has been taken dreadful advantage of."

A couple of hours later, a much-changed Tom was brought up to her office. He had gorged himself on bread and jam until he declared, "me breadbasket won't take no more," and had then been sized up for clothing and led away to a bathtub of warm water. Mrs. Hancock had judged rightly that he might have objections to being stripped and washed, so she had commissioned two of the younger footmen to stand by. Young Tom fought like a cat, raging that he had already washed his dabbers and phiz (interpreted by one of the footmen, who was a Londoner, as his hands and face) and he "weren't goin' to get in no bath for nobody." It took both of the footmen to hold him down while Mrs. Hancock scrubbed off what she could of the dirt. She washed his hair but certain it was full of lice, decided she would have to shave his head. That took a third footman. They were all exhausted and soaked from head to foot by the end of the exercise and Tom was very much inclined to cry.

However, one of the maids who had younger brothers at home had been dispatched to purchase a complete set of clothing for him, including socks, boots and a cloth cap, and when he was dried and dressed in these, he was very much happier. He looked a different person. He was by no means ill-favored, with bright blue eyes and when not howling imprecations against those around him, a pleasant face. Mrs. Hancock observed that the hair lying on the floor was drying quite fair, a fact that had been indiscernible before. When his bald head was covered with the cap, he looked quite handsome.

Presenting him to Amelia, Mrs. Hancock said in a low voice that it had quite turned her stomach to see the bruises and scars the poor boy had on his back. She wondered there were such monsters in the world who would beat a child so.

"Have no fear, whoever it was will do it no more," said Miss Moreton, with such a martial light in her eye that the housekeeper had no trouble believing her.

Chapter Ten

All Tom could tell her about the location of the factory was that it was "that way, down by the river," so she set out with him in a hackney towards the East End of London. It was not an area Amelia knew at all. Since living with her aunt, she had never been further east than Hyde Park, where she and her brother had occasionally had a gallop on hired horses. However, these were such sluggards that neither of them had enjoyed it very much.

As they were conveyed east, the sights and sounds of London changed. From the elegant porticoed mansions of Mayfair, they drove through the streets of the more modest establishments of the merely well-to-do, which Amelia knew quite well, past the homes of tradespeople and merchants, into the din and stink of the city. Here, the filthy and crowded habitations tumbled next to the warehouses and foundries serving the docks, and every third establishment appeared to be a public house. The smell of open sewers and rotting cargo was almost overpowering.

For a while, Tom, hanging out of the window enjoying the first ride he had ever taken in a horse-drawn vehicle, did not know where he was. When he had run away it had been dark, and though he knew the area immediately around the factory where he lived and worked, he knew little else. He had simply set his face in the direction someone had once told him was "up west" and run or walked and then finally dragged himself all night, until he came to where Amelia had found him. When questioned, he said the place was near the river and had big chimneys, so the hackney driver was ordered to just stay as close as he could to the water until Tom recognized something.

Amelia knew they had come to the place when she felt his hand steal into hers. She squeezed it and said, "Do not fear, Tom," she said, "I won't let anyone hurt you." They had stopped outside the iron gates of a long brick building, with, as Tom had said, chimneys belching smoke into the air. A smell akin to wet washing hung in the air.

Telling the hackney to wait, she walked boldly into the building with Tom close behind her. The noise was deafening and a white fibrous dust filled the air, catching in her throat and making her blink. It was also very hot. Then she saw a portly individual in a dirty waistcoat standing on a platform a few feet above the level of the machine and climbed the steps up to him. Tom hung back, his head down, as if he were fearful of being recognized. When she got to the platform she could see that white balls not unlike mounds of mashed potato were being fed into the machine below, emerging as a thick mat with a few brown specks in it. Two children of about Tom's size were picking at it on either side. The mat passed between two rollers and came out as a white ribbon. The ribbon disappeared towards the other end of the machine. Between the distance and the white haze that hung over everything, she could not see what happened to it after that. She did not know what the product was, but guessed from the smell that it was cotton. It smelled like the laundry room after the ironing was done.

The portly individual looked taken aback and came towards her, an enquiring look on his face. He clearly did not recognize Tom. Amelia tried to talk to him, but the din made it impossible. Finally, she started back down the few steps and beckoned imperiously for him to follow her. Tom came slowly after them both, his eyes still on the ground. She led the man outside and turned to face him. He was a middle-aged person of about the same height as she, but when she looked down her nose at him, he had the impression he was nothing but a grubby schoolboy.

"Tom," she said, "is this the man who beat you?"

"Yes, Miss," answered Tom in a low voice. "That's old Skillins."

The sound of his name made the man narrow his eyes. "Tom?" he looked at the boy who turned his bright blue eyes on him for the first time. "By God, it is! You come 'ere boy! What are you doing with them togs on? You nab 'em from this lady? I'm sorry, Madam," he spread his hands in a conciliatory gesture, "'E's a terrible little thief. 'E'll 'ave yer coat of yer back if you don't watch 'im. You get over 'ere right now, or I'll skin yer 'ide."

"I think you have already done that more than once, Mr. Skillins," said Amelia, looking at that individual as if he were the dirt on her shoe, "My name is Amelia Moreton. I am secretary to the Earl of Ailesbury. What is your relationship with Tom here?" The haughtiness of her tone plus the mention of nobility had the effect of forcing an answer from the man.

"Relationship? Why... I don't...," he stammered. "'Is Pa left 'im 'ere when 'e were a nipper. I've fed 'im and clothed 'im and...."

"Did his father give you some sort of payment in return for your goodness to his son?"

"Payment? Not bloody likely, excusing me, your ladyship. It were t'other way round! I give 'im £20 for the boy."

"You mean you bought this child from his father? Do you realize that the selling of children is illegal in this country? But I am assuming you know this and have therefore regarded Tom in the light of apprentice for these last years. May I see the terms of his indenture?"

Since Mr. Skillins had never regarded Tom in any light at all except as someone to be worked like a mule and beaten like one, he looked around wildly for whatever he could say or do to make this dreadful woman stop talking and go away. Quite a crowd had gathered.

"Very well, I shall look around inside and see if you have more slaves in your possession."

Amelia stalked into the factory and walked around the full perimeter of the awful, clattering machine. What she saw shocked her as nothing had ever done before. Children she judged to be as young as four or five were working under and around some sort of monstrous shuddering bed. At the end nearest the overseer's platform was a row of bobbins holding the wide ribbon she had previously observed.

"Them's rovings, Miss," explained Tom. "They 'as to get thinned out and wound on the spindles."

They were evidently beginning a new batch. At the far end women were packing wound spindles of cotton into square baskets and rapidly reloading empty ones onto the machine. The empty spindles were laid flat and children were pulling the ends of the roving ribbon to them and attaching them. Then behind them, a wooden bar came down to hold the ribbon securely, the spindles were locked upright and moved back, so that it was pulled taut. A lever was pulled and the clattering monster sprang into life. The spindles rotated, twisting and winding the cotton ribbon into thread. When one length of thread had been spun, the bar was raised and more roving released, in one continuous movement. If one of the threads broke, which was a frequent

66

occurrence as the fibers in cotton are very short, a child would reach among the moving parts and quickly wind it back together. Amelia shuddered to think how many of those little fingers had been broken and mangled by that awful machine. The children were all covered in white dust, like ghostly little creatures from some hellish underworld. She had once seen a representation of Hades in an illuminated medieval manuscript in the British Library. This looked worse: these blind-looking little creatures working without speaking, looking at nothing but the endless string of ribbon that poured inexorably from the bobbins.

She walked around the other side of the rattling contraption and at the other end beyond the overseer's platform, women were loading the white balls of what Amelia now realized was raw cotton into the machine she had observed from the platform. The balls passed through a machine like a giant comb that flattened them into the mat she had previously observed. The children she had seen before were picking seeds out from the mass as it emerged.

"That's the carding, Miss," shouted Tom. "It's s'pposed to get all the seeds out, but some gets though 'an we 'as to pick 'em out. I used to do that job when I got too big to get under the spinner."

"Do all these children belong to Mr. Skillins?" Amelia shouted back.

"No, Miss. They works alongside their Ma mostly. They goes 'ome once it gets too dark. I was the only one wot stayed 'ere."

"Where did you sleep?"

"In the corner over there." He indicated a dark hole where a pile of what looked like sacks was heaped up. 'E locked me in at night. It weren't too bad except for the rats. It were the beatings when 'e'd 'ad one too many got to me. 'E lives next door, and when he got tired of beating 'is missus, he'd come after me. And I were always 'ungry."

Amelia had seen all there was to see, or all she could bear to see. She returned to Mr. Skillins.

"I take it you are the overseer of this… establishment. Who is the owner?"

"Me Lord Smithson is the owner. 'E bought the machinery somewhere up north and 'ad it brought down 'ere. Only cotton factory in London! We gets the water for the steam from the river and the cotton goes to the weavers down in Spitalfields. Most of 'em does silk, but we got one does cotton. A very fine product, we make too," he ended on a note of pride.

"Did Lord Smithson approve of your… purchase of Tom?"

"Now, look 'ere, your ladyship, I didn't…."

"Did he?"

"No, 'e didn't know nuffin' about it."

"I'm glad to hear it. A peer of the realm aiding and abetting child slavery is something the newspapers would be very interested in." She looked at him, her eyes hard. "I am also sure they would find the shocking conditions in this mill something to report on. The floor is inches deep in cotton dust. Breathing in the atmosphere for just a few minutes has injured my throat. I cannot imagine what it does to those poor women and children who work in it all day. I wonder what the papers will report when I inform them of the name of the noble owner. I recommend you clean it up before they get here."

She swept out into the yard. "I'm taking Tom back with me. You may consider yourself lucky I don't pursue this in the courts.

You have kept him here against his will and used him as a slave. As far as I can tell, he had never been paid for his work. If you should ever come near him or harm him in any way, I shall not only undertake prosecution but make sure Lord Smithson's name is associated with it. I cannot imagine that would be to his liking."

"Bless you, your ladyship, you take 'im an' welcome. A lazy, good-for-nothing boy 'e is. I'm well shut of 'im."

"Good, then my business here is done. Good day, Mr. Skillins. Come, Tom."

She climbed into the waiting hackney, Tom, hardly able to believe his good luck, running close behind her, leaving Mr. Skillins mopping his overheated brow. Once the overseer had calmed down, however, he put on his hat and coat and visited Lord Smithson in his sumptuous Mayfair home. He told him all about Miss Amelia Moreton, Secretary to The Earl of Ailesbury, and her threat to contact the newspapers. She had also stolen one of his best workers, a boy he'd looked after like a son. The net result was that the mill lost a day of production as the machines were silenced while, to keep the dust down, the floors were sprinkled with water and swept out. The visit from the newspaper reporters never materialized and my Lord Smithson was left to rage inwardly that not only had he been made a fool of, but he'd lost a day's profit. He vowed revenge on that red-headed busybody.

The busybody's ride back to Albemarle Street was accomplished in almost total silence, each in contemplation of the future. Tom was wondering if he might get any more bread and jam, but Miss Moreton's thoughts ran on very different lines. She did not for a moment consider what Mr. Skillins might do about her threats or her taking Tom. She had been shocked to her core by what she had seen at the factory. In the country some families had been poor, but at least their children were in the fresh air. She had never envisioned that was what urban poverty looked like: mothers and their children working in such shocking conditions, unhealthy and dangerous for them all. Where were the men? In her world, it was the men who provided for the women and children.

"Do those women have husbands, Tom? Do the children have fathers?"

"I s'pose so, but men don't work in the fact'ry, Miss! Spinnin' is wimmen's work! Anyway, they's prob'ly down the pub at this hour."

Amelia understood now why there were knots of men on the street corners or outside the pubs they had passed. She reflected that women had ever been the ones to bear the chief burden of looking after the children, even in the class of society she inhabited. Would it always be like that, she wondered?

Her thoughts returned to the awful sight she had seen. Children that young should not be working at all, and especially not in such conditions! It was not unreasonable for the mothers to take their young children with them, she supposed, but they should not be under and around those dangerous machines. What education could they possibly be receiving? Could any of them read or write? If not, it would mean when they grew up they would be relegated to the same sort of work, and the cycle would begin again. Something had to be done.

Chapter Eleven

This time when she got back to Albemarle Street, she took Tom with her through the front door.

"Bullock," she said, in her most quelling style, forestalling any objections he might voice, "this is Tom. You told me some time ago that the footman in charge of delivering notes and such had more work than he could handle. Tom will take over some of it. He may take Tom with him for the next couple of weeks to show him where things are and how to go on, then Tom will take over that function. He will need suitable livery, of course, but I'm sure you will see to that. Tom, make your bow to Mr. Bullock. He is your new overseer."

Tom had never been directed to bow before and had no idea how to go about it, so he bobbed his head rather as if he were trying to bite an apple in a barrel.

"No, you will bow from the waist, Tom, and remove your cap when you are in the house."

"But Miss, me 'ead 'll be cold. I ain't got no 'air no more!"

"Nonetheless, you will remove your cap and bow from the waist to Mr. Bullock."

Tom pulled off his cap with a scowl and gave an exaggeratedly deep bow, almost touching his nose to his knees.

"Tom!" said Amelia sternly. "Look at me! If you do not behave you will not get your dinner! Bow just low enough that you can see the bottom of Mr. Bullock's waistcoat. If you should happen to meet his lordship or any ladies other than myself, which I doubt, you will bow a few inches lower. But any exaggerated performance is at all times forbidden. This is a gentleman's household and his servants will behave with propriety."

Whether it was because Miss Moreton had for the first time spoken severely to him or the threat of a lack of dinner, Tom complied and achieved a creditable bow. Before the butler could say anything, Amelia whisked the boy downstairs, and asked Annie to give him whatever was left of the servants' dinner. She then explained to Mrs. Hancock what she had seen at the factory.

"I couldn't leave him there, Mrs. Hancock, I simply could not," she cried. "I wish I could have saved all the children, but they had their mothers. Tom had no one at all to take care of him. Now, do you have a bed he can sleep in and jobs for him to do? I propose giving him a shilling a week to spend and putting aside a pound a month for when he is a man. If he works well, as he grows I will see to it that his wages increase to those of a footman, which I hope he will turn out to be. I think him not ill-favored, and good looks are important in a footman, are they not?"

"Oh, Miss, there are a thousand jobs always needing doing. We lost our boot-boy, for one thing. He went off to live with his sister when she got married, to help on the farm. To tell the truth, I've been too busy with the spring cleaning to look for a new one. And he used to share a room with young Alf, so Tom can go in there with him. That bed's available. Now, I won't have any shirking, mind. I'll take the back of my hairbrush to his hindquarters if I have to, for all that's he's a favorite of yours."

Amelia laughed. "He's not a favorite. I just think he deserves a better life than the one he had. I trust you to keep an eye on him."

So Tom slid joyfully into life at number 23 Albemarle Street. He had never slept in a bed before, and when he woke up between sheets had to pinch himself to remember where he was. He ate every scrap of food put in front of him, and if anyone left something on the plate, he ate that too. In spite of his cruel upbringing, he was a cheerful boy. He whistled as he polished the boots or sauntered down the streets of Mayfair delivering the messages and notes from number 23. As his hair began to grow in, it was indeed quite fair and flopped engagingly over his forehead. Mrs. Hancock, never having had children of her own, never in fact having been married (the Mrs. was a courtesy title accorded to all housekeepers), took him under her wing and began to teach him to read and write. He couldn't believe he was actually being paid to live a life he enjoyed. The only thing he still disliked intensely was washing every day and the weekly bathing he was forced to endure. The only way he could be brought to perform these tasks was by telling him that Miss Moreton wanted him to do it. She was the angel who had delivered him from hell and taken him up to heaven. With his first week's shilling he bought a bunch of violets he placed on her desk. When she kissed his cheek in thanks, he thought his heart would explode. Soon he discovered the stables in the mews behind the house and when his duties were done, he spent the lengthening evenings there. It became his favorite place. It seemed he loved and had a way with horses.

Amelia was well satisfied with the outcome concerning Tom. He was proving a useful addition to the household and since he had replaced the boot boy, the staff's wages saw no change. She saw no reason to tell the Earl she had hired a very junior person. But the vision she had seen in the cotton mill never left her.

She had rarely read The Times before coming to work at number 23, but now she had taken to glancing at it once his lordship had finished. It was interesting to see names she recognized from her employer's correspondence appearing now and then, especially in the Court Circular. The Earl had dined at the Urquharts' a few weeks previously, soon after Lord Urquhart had assumed the title upon the death of his father. Then one day she saw a report of the same lord's Maiden Speech in the House of Lords. He had spoken about trade with the now independent America, which, he was glad to report, was now back at the same levels it had been twenty-five years before. Since he seemed to have listed the hundredweights of a huge list of products, it must have been the dullest speech imaginable. But Amelia knew it was a courtesy of the House that a Maiden Speech was never interrupted, so people must have sat through it, willy-nilly. She would ask the Earl what he had thought of his friend's first effort.

The opportunity came the following day, when her employer came into her office unexpectedly.

"Miss Moreton!" he said, "Your assumption of my affairs has been so complete that I never see you these days! Whatever I pay you, it cannot be enough! Give yourself a raise!"

"That is quite unnecessary, my lord," smiled Amelia. "I like to be busy. But since you are here, may I ask you a question?"

Receiving an affirmative "of course", she continued, "Did you hear Lord Urquhart's Maiden Speech about trade with America? It was reported in The Times. I know he is a friend of yours, so forgive me for saying it, but it sounds as though it was dreadfully dull."

"Urquhart's speech?" his lordship looked astonished. "Why ever should you think I heard that?"

"Well, he is a friend of yours, and it was his Maiden Speech. I thought you might have been there to support him."

"Good God, no! I cannot conceive of anything more deadly. I only go into the House when I'm sure of entertainment. I like to go when the subject under debate is so contentious the Honorable Members would kill each other if the Leader didn't intervene."

"What did you talk about in your Maiden Speech?"

"Nothing. I haven't made one. Why should I? There's enough speechifying without me! I told you, I stay away as much as possible."

Amelia sat bolt upright. An idea had occurred to her. But not one she would at the moment reveal to her employer. "I see," she said neutrally. "I thought it was required of all Members. I suppose if one chooses to make a speech, one has to have oneself put on the calendar?"

"No, it's not required to make a speech, but I imagine if one does, a calendar is involved. Why? Are you planning to make one there yourself?" He laughed. "If any woman could do it, you could."

She laughed heartily. "No, my lord, I'm much too busy with your affairs."

"In that case," he replied with his charming smile, "I shall leave you in case you find something for me to do. Good day, Miss Moreton. But you should give yourself that raise."

He bowed and was gone.

Chapter Twelve

Hearing that her employer had yet to give his Maiden Speech in the House of Lords, Amelia had instantly decided that whether he wanted to or not, he would give his first speech and he would talk about child labor. She was sure that if he was committed to a thing, his honor as a gentleman would not allow him to withdraw at the last minute. She just had to get him on the calendar and not tell him till it was too late for him to withdraw. He had gone to that balloon ascension with the whey-faced maiden, after all, in spite of complaining about it. Of his own admission he hardly ever went near the House, so he was unlikely to find out he was on the calendar.

She was so convinced of the need for action on this question that all her plans for Aurelius took a second place. She thought it quite likely she would lose her position when her employer found out what she had done. She just had to hope that, having met her brother, the Earl would do what he could for him for his own sake, rather than for hers. But the sooner it was done, the better. She decided the best moment for the speech was between Easter and Whitsun. At Whitsun the Lords would disappear to their estates and might not return to London all summer, except for Ascot at the end of the month. That year Easter was on 26th of March and Whitsun was 4th of June. It was already the middle of March, so she had to work swiftly.

She knew full well what she was doing was most outrageously improper. It would certainly anger her employer, but what could he do, after all, other than dismiss her? Tossing her red mane and setting her chin, she drew out a piece of his lordship's elegant stationary. Having seen the name in The Times on a number of occasions, she knew Lord Liverpool was the Leader of the House. It was to him she wrote.

Albemarle Street, London
The 15th of March, 1815
My dear Liverpool,

My attention has been drawn to the appalling use of child labor, the children sometimes as young as four or five, by a cotton mill in the East End of London. The hellish conditions there are no doubt replicated in manufactories across the country. The Factories Act passed some thirteen years ago did not even attempt to address this issue. I would like to use the occasion of my Maiden Speech to bring to the attention of my peers this heathenish practice, unworthy of our great nation.

I hold myself at your disposal for any date and time between Easter and Whitsun.

Yours, etc.
Ailesbury

She scrawled the signature as she had seen her employer many times. She put the letter in an envelope, tucked it in her reticule, pinned her hair firmly out of sight under her uncompromising bonnet and set out for the House of Lords.

She entered the new House of Lords building constructed in the neo-gothic style about twenty years before. She had read it was scathingly called The Cotton Mill, which she found singularly appropriate. Women were rare in those august chambers and she drew a number of curious glances. But she marched steadfastly forward and by dint of asking help of anyone she saw, was able to find her way. She passed the desks of a number of grey little men until she finally arrived at the greyest of the lot, the secretary to the Leader himself. He was a round-shouldered individual whose age was impossible to determine. His suit looked dusty. In fact everything about him looked dusty, apart from a shining bald head plastered over with a few strands of faded hair. He wore a pince-nez and the put-upon expression that told her he must be one of those who either performed, or thought they performed, a great deal of unappreciated work. She set herself to charm him. She commiserated with him on the difficulties of persuading subordinates to mend their nibs regularly, the poor quality of ink that these days invariably turned to mud in the bottom of the bottle, and the lack of attention one's superiors paid to one's efforts.

She found out from him that any lord sitting in the benches must have been introduced to the House, taken the Oath and signed the Register. Since the Earl had said he did occasionally attend sessions, he must have already completed these requirements. As to the management of the House Calendar, she said she had no idea how anyone could keep it all straight. It must be dreadfully complicated! She was sure the gentlemen changed their minds all the time! The person who managed it must be so clever, and have the patience of a saint, besides. It was he who managed it? No! She had no idea she was talking to such an important individual! The Leader simply passed the requests along to him and he arranged it all? Good gracious! How lucky she was to have met such an important man as he! Might she look at the Calendar? It would be such a treat to see it!

Dazzled by this wave of complimentary eloquence, the man willingly opened a huge register covered in red leather embossed in gold with the legend: 1815. Amelia turned over the pages and discovered that a name had been crossed through at eleven o'clock in the morning on Thursday 13th April.

"Tell me, sir, this name seems to have been removed. Is this spot therefore free?"

The grey little man bent his head myopically over the page. "Hmpf… yes, it appears so. Why?"

"Well, sir, you will think me most awfully stupid, and indeed I am," said Amelia earnestly. "You see, I am… er, housekeeper to Lord Ailesbury. Some weeks ago I was just leaving to go out and he asked me to put this out for delivery." She produced the letter from her reticule. "He said I should congratulate him because he'd decided to make his Maiden Speech in the House of Lords. But," her lip quivered, "I put it in my coat pocket and forgot it. I just discovered it this morning. I don't usually wear this coat, you see. Oh, sir!" her eyes filled with tears, "If you could put him in where this name is crossed out, he need never know! I'm afraid I'll lose my position otherwise, sir! I heard him shouting at his secretary this morning about why he hadn't received an answer from the House. That's what put me in mind of it."

"That would be most irregular! I don't think…."

"But sir, you said Lord Liverpool just hands the requests to you. You do all the work! Please sir, if I lose my position I don't know what I'll do. My Jimmy, he was wounded in the Peninsular War, you see, and…." Tears dropped from her eyes.

What could the poor man do? Embarrassed by having a comely young woman weeping over him, her husband wounded in the service of his country, and seeing in her someone as oppressed as himself, he found himself agreeing. He took a (well-mended) pen, and carefully wrote *Earl of Ailesbury: Md. Sp. Child Labor* over the original crossed-out name.

"C...can you write the answer to the letter n... now, sir?" she stuttered. "Th... that way I'll p... put in in his post and he won't be any the... the wiser."

Resigned, the clerk drew out a card emblazoned with House of Lords, and wrote in a beautiful hand:

> *The Right Honorable the Earl of Ailesbury*
> *Has Been Placed on the Calendar*
> *To Address his Maiden Speech to the House on*
> *Thursday the 13th of April, 1815*
> *At 11 o'clock in the Morning.*
> *(signed) R.T. Boothroyd, Secy. to the Leader*

He liberally sprinkled it with sand, shook it off, placed it in an envelope and gave it to her.

"Oh, sir!" Amelia made as if to kiss his hand, but he hastily withdrew it, saying, "Most irregular, most irregular."

She gratified him with a curtsey, saying, in all truth, "I'll never forget your kindness, sir," and quickly withdrew.

It was typical of Amelia that once she had arranged a thing, she spent no time worrying about it, but passed on to more immediate issues. The speech was barely a month away, but in between came Easter. His lordship had already told her that he would be going home to Deering, his estate in Hertfordshire. He wanted to spend the holiday with his mother and enjoy the last hunt of the season. He would be gone for two weeks and wanted her to come with him. He said it was because he often had business at home she could help him with, but it was really because he wanted his mother, herself a very decided woman, to meet Amelia. He wondered what she would make of her. And besides, though he did not admit it to himself, he wanted to see more of her.

Amelia agreed to go with him. In her case, however, the reason she gave herself kept her conscience clear. She had been thinking about the management of his lordship's estates. Once she had the household expenses under control and could deal with her employer's correspondence without difficulty, she had begun to wonder about the estate accounts. These would only come in at the end of the first quarter, but she was interested enough to find the records of previous quarters in the drawers where her predecessor had placed them. She quickly saw the enormous income his lordship derived from his estate, both in revenue from the lands under his direct control (or rather, that of his land manager), and from the tenancy payments collected by his agent. She also saw the huge outgoings on repairs to the cottages and other areas in the estate.

Curious, she unearthed the accounts from the previous five years and saw that essentially the same repairs were being undertaken year after year, without there being any real long-term improvement. Roofs leaked and were patched; walls fell down and were put up again, only to fall a year or so later; the timber framing of two-hundred-year-old lath and plaster cottages rotted and was replaced haphazardly; the river flooded some of the dwellings every spring. Amelia wondered why more permanent repairs had not been undertaken. She resolved to talk to his lordship about it while they were driving to Deering. She realized, with more of a pang than she wanted to admit, that this trip might be one of the last times she would have a chance of friendly conversation with him. Once he knew what she had done in the matter of his Maiden Speech, he would probably never speak to her again.

She explained to Aurelius she would not be going home with him for the last hunt of the season, and encouraged him to go on his own. She thought he would be glad of the chance for exercise and the outdoors, but he surprised her by saying he would stay in London.

"I'm promised to some jolly good fellows for a romp here and there. Places where you see a slice of life, not where you could go, of course! And I want to keep up my sparring practice at Gentleman Jackson's. Saw your man there, the other day, by the way."

"If by my man you mean the Earl," she answered with a laugh, "I hope you made your bow to him. You owe him a good deal for the introduction there."

"Good Lord, yes, I said everything pretty and asked him how you were gettin' along."

"You didn't! What did he say?"

"Said he didn't know how he got along without you. Asked me if you bully me as much as you bully him! 'Course I said you've bullied me since the day I was born, because you came out first!"

"Aury! How could you? I don't bully you! You know I never interfere... unless it's for your own good."

"You probably think it's for his own good, too! He strips to advantage, I must say. Fine looking fellow and what a boxer! Saw him in the ring with the Champion. Came as near as dammit to landing him one, but Jackson nipped one in under his guard at the last moment."

"He didn't hurt him?" Amelia felt a sudden pang. She was bullying her employer, she knew, and the worst was still to come. But she didn't like to think of that laughing, carefree individual actually being hurt.

"Lord, no! You have to pull your punches. It's a rule. No harm done."

"Well, if you stay in London," said his sister, coming back to the original point of their discussion, "don't do anything foolish! You've been out late nearly every night this week. Every time you think of doing a thing, ask yourself if I would approve. If you can't answer honestly yes, don't do it!"

"And you say you don't bully me!" Aurelius exclaimed. "If I asked myself that every time, I wouldn't do anything!"

He caught her around the waist and kissed her soundly on the cheek. "What about you? Don't you do anything with that Earl of yours I wouldn't approve of. Remember, I'm the head of the family."

Amelia found herself blushing. "Whatever can you mean? He's my employer. He doesn't even think of me as a woman. I told him not to!"

"Not a woman! What are you thinking of, Amy? You most certainly are a woman, and a damn fine-looking one. If he don't think so, he must be an odd customer, and from what I hear, he ain't. Likes an armful as much as the next man."

"Well, I am not his armful, if that's what you're implying," retorted his sister. "I'm very sure he doesn't think of me in that way at all. And I most definitely do not think of him like that either."

But as she lay in bed that night, her thoughts returning to the conversation, she knew she hadn't told her brother the whole truth. She had come to realize that on the days she did not see her employer, and since she dealt so effectively with his affairs, they were many, she went home with an odd sense of disappointment. The realization both surprised and troubled her.

Chapter Thirteen

Anyone seeing young Tom the first day he had arrived at number 23 Albemarle Street and seeing him now would not have recognized him. The copious amount of food he consumed had filled out his frame, though he was still small and slight. His face had lost the starved look and his bright blue eyes gleamed on the world with unfailing good humor. His fair, flat hair had grown in and flopped in his eyes no matter how often Mrs. Hancock cut it. At first, he had been terrified of making a mistake. Once, when he inadvertently brought dirt into the kitchen from the stables, where he spent all the time he could, he cowered with his arms over his head, expecting to be beaten. When Mrs. Hancock simply told him to clean it up and be more careful next time, he put his arms down and looked around in amazement, before scuttling off to do as he had been told. After that, he became preoccupied with the cleanliness of his clothing, puzzling the staff by asking for a belly cheat, which no one understood until the young London-bred footman explained it was an apron. He wore this item whenever he was below stairs, so his livery was always spotless.

One morning just before Easter as she was approaching number 23, Amelia saw a handsome curricle and pair in front of the door. An admiring Tom was standing nearby. Just then, a dog ran across the road barking and chasing a terrified squirrel that ran between the hooves of the matched chestnuts. The horse closest to the pavement reared up in fright, the groom dropped the reins and the animal would have caused either itself or its partner injury, had Tom not run immediately up front. Braving the wildly pawing hooves, he caught hold of the rearing horse's bridle, all the while talking incomprehensibly in a soothing language that the horse apparently understood. It quickly calmed down and stood quietly, its head bowed next to Tom's as the boy continued to murmur into its ear. The squirrel and the dog both disappeared.

"Who is that boy?" asked the Earl, who had come out of the house in time to see the whole episode.

"It's Tom," said Amelia, a little out of breath, as she had run down the street, "He's the... the new boot boy."

"He's wasted as a boot boy," said her employer. "I've never seen a lad deal with a frightened horse like that. I had a feeling those chestnuts are a little too high strung for city use."

He beckoned to Tom, who came over and executed a bow exactly as Amelia had instructed him.

"Thank you, Tom," said the Earl. "You saved me a great deal of trouble, not to say expense. Where did you learn to deal with horses like that?"

"I dunno yer Honor," answered Tom. "I just likes 'orses and they likes me. Now Jenny there, she don't like a shock. Noticed it before when someone dropped a bucket o' water on the stones on the yard. But she's a good 'orse."

"That she is. But it seems to me you should do more than polish boots. I need a Tiger. To ride up behind the curricle, you understand. What do you say to changing professions?"

"You mean ride up there?" he indicated the small seat at the back of the curricle.

"Yes, and hold the horses when needed."

"Cor blimey! Yes, yer Honor."

"You must call his lordship my lord," whispered Amelia.

"Yes, me lord," said Tom reverently.

"Then it's settled. Miss Moreton, please settle with Bullock about boots and new livery for the boy."

With that, his lordship sprang up into the driving seat, took the reins from the waiting groom and departed at a sprightly trot. Amelia stood looking wistfully after him, not at the Earl, but at the curricle and pair. How she missed driving a spirited team! She sighed and went inside.

When Amelia turned up on the morning on their departure for Deering with nothing but a small trunk, the Earl's eyebrows went up.

"Is that all you're bringing, Miss Moreton?" he asked in surprise.

"Yes, apart from a couple of day dresses, the only other thing I brought was my riding habit. I hoped," she explained a little bashfully, "that I might be permitted to hunt, if your lordship has a horse I might ride."

The Earl naturally had a well-stocked stable, but since his mother no longer rode, all his animals were bought for him and he doubted whether any would suit a lady. He said so.

"Oh, I don't mind an animal with spirit," she said. "And my brother and I grew up more or less exchanging horses until well after he became taller and heavier than I. I don't mind riding above my weight. If your lordship would care to try me out, you will see."

"Very well, Miss Moreton, but I don't care to see you come to grief. It's not so much the horse, but you I fear for. I shall never again find such an excellent secretary." He smiled at her, and her heart gave a leap.

It turned out they were to take the curricle, with a carriage behind for the Earl's valet and the luggage. Amelia quickly made it clear she would rather ride in the curricle than the carriage, and so they set off, Tom perched behind with a wide smile on his face. It had been explained he was to blow the horn, or yard of tin as it was called, to summon the turnpike fee collectors so that they would not be unduly held up. He could hardly wait to perform this office and together with the fact he had never before been out of London before, he was so excited he could scarcely breathe.

A curricle is not the best place to try to have a business discussion and the Earl of Ailesbury not the best person with whom to try to have a discussion at any time. Miss Moreton had brought with her the facts and figures she had gleaned from her examination of the estate accounts, but did not think she could begin talking about them immediately. Instead she complimented her employer on his horses, and talked so knowledgeably about their points that he looked at her in some surprise. Then, having left the outskirts of London, he let his hands drop and the lively chestnuts leaped forward at full gallop. Amelia's exhilaration was such that all thoughts of business fled from her mind. Her bright red hair flew from under her bonnet and her countenance glowed.

"You obviously enjoy a good gallop, Miss Moreton," he shouted in her ear.

"Yes, indeed I do! I used to frighten all the grooms when I was younger!" she shouted back.

When the Earl judged the fidgets had been galloped out of his horses, he drew them into a steady trot and conversation was much easier.

"So I gather you can drive a pair, Miss Moreton?" said the Earl. "Would you care to drive these?"

Amelia's eyes when she turned to him sparkled with such anticipation that no answer was necessary. He drew the horses to a halt and jumped down. She moved over and he took her place.

"But, I warn you," he said, "if I think you are causing the slightest damage to the chestnuts' mouths, I shall stop you with no apology."

"If I damage their mouths to the slightest degree, you have my permission not only to stop me but to throw me off the curricle," she retorted, a light kindling in her eye.

He laughed and sat back to watch her as she set the chestnuts in motion. Her handling of the reins was light and sure. She was perfectly at ease, and once she had established a rapport with the horses, she too sat back.

"You handle the cattle remarkably well for a woman," remarked her passenger.

"I handle them remarkably well for anybody," she replied tartly. "My brother will tell you I can out drive and out ride him on any and all occasions."

"You don't box, too, do you?" he asked with a grin.

"No! My mother wouldn't let me!" she smiled back." But I fence. Not as well as Aurelius, though. He is very good."

"He shows promise as a boxer, I've seen him. Good science and intelligent."

"He told me he'd seen you at Gentleman Jackson's." She suddenly threw caution to the winds. "You like him, don't you?"

"Like him?" the Earl turned inquiring eyes on her. "I don't know him very well, but I like what I see. Of course, it's hard not to like someone who looks the way he does." He smiled, wondering where this was heading. He soon found out.

"If the opportunity arose, would you help him?"

"Help him in what way? Is he in trouble? He didn't appear to be the last time I saw him."

"No," she said with a smile of her own. "He's not in trouble, it's just that...,"she hesitated, "that he wants to go into the army. He talks of nothing else. But he's so biddable, I just know he would get wounded or killed. I want him to be in the Diplomatic Service. He's so good looking and," she burst out, "such a good person. I know that would be the best for him. And for me. He's all I have, you see."

"Does he want to be a diplomat?"

"He hasn't said he doesn't. He didn't make a fuss when I told him he couldn't go into the army. But he never fusses. I told you, he's so good. I understand your brother-in-law is in Vienna. Couldn't you encourage him to take Aury on?"

"I'm not sure I have any influence with my brother-in-law. I'm sorry to say he thinks me a useless fellow. His opinion of me is probably not much better than yours."

"What can you mean? I don't have a poor opinion of you! Whatever makes you think that?"

"You are constantly taxing me with things I've overlooked. No!" he smiled at her as she began to protest, "do not deny it! You know what I am!"

When she thought how she had brought papers with her to show him how to run his estate more efficiently, she had to admit, she did know what he was. To hide her confusion, she said, "Do you think the chestnuts are rested enough now, sir? Might we have a gallop?"

"By all means, Miss Moreton. It seems galloping horses is something we can agree on!"

So Amelia dropped her hands and the chestnuts sprang forward. She had to concentrate now, and all other thoughts were chased from her mind. The Earl watched her with appreciation. She was absolutely in control of his horses and drove with the perfect combination of relaxation and attention. Her handling of the reins was calm and sure. The horses recognized a master and moved with swift confidence. For the first time he could remember while his horses were being driven by someone else, he simply sat back and let his mind wander. It wandered to the enigma that was his secretary. He had wondered why she was working for him. She was obviously a gentlewoman by upbringing and education. Though she did not wear fashionable clothing, her brother most certainly did. So it was not a question of money. Now he thought he understood: he was to be a conduit for her brother.

He did not think he could help him. What he had told her about his relationship with his brother-in law was true; the man thought him a worthless fribble and was bound to think anyone he recommended as bad as himself. In any case, it did not seem Aurelius had any particular liking for the Diplomatic Service. It was his sister who wanted it for him. But if he let her down, would she find another employer to further her brother's career? He would hate to lose her, and not only because she was the best secretary he had ever had. His home ran more smoothly than ever before. He had been accustomed to his housekeeper or his butler approaching him from time to time on matters of a domestic nature. He never paid a great deal of attention to their usually exhaustive explanations but simply agreed with whatever they suggested at the end. Now he never saw them. Everyone recognized in Miss Moreton his lordship's proxy: the person who would not only listen but also probably propose a better solution.

As far as his social engagements went, things had never been smoother. He had been appreciated for his swift response to an invitation he had never even seen, but would have gladly accepted if he had; he had been thanked by a remote acquaintance for an expression of sympathy he didn't remember writing; a young lady whose mother had been an intimate of his own had expressed gratitude for a book of illustrated quotations he had sent her for her birthday. This had been a stroke of genius on Miss Moreton's part. It was both impersonal and pretty. The maiden could not complain, but neither could she imagine it was in any way an expression of anything more than mild friendship. He had commented on this to his secretary. Her response was characteristic.

"Oh that," she said. "Yes, I thought it might improve her mind. To judge from how most of these young ladies seem to carry on, she probably needs it."

Yes, he thought. Miss Moreton was in every respect an excellent secretary.

But he knew, in his heart of hearts, this was not the reason he would hate to lose her. He had never known a woman less intent on engaging his attentions, or one who engaged him more. She had a sharp tongue, but it was accompanied by a ready wit that entranced him. The house was a good-humored place with her in it. She said exactly what she thought to everyone, but no one took offence, any more than he did himself. He had at first thought her merely pleasant looking. Now he saw she had an unusual beauty, with that wild mane of red hair. She swept through the house like a whirlwind, her curls usually flying behind her, no matter how often she tried to pin them up. Looking at her now, he faced the truth: she fascinated him. There she was, driving his chestnuts as well as he drove them himself and without the slightest attempt at coquetry. She was not doing it because she wanted him to think well of her. She was doing it because it was what she loved.

His lordship was, of course, mistaken in his belief that Miss Moreton thought of him as nothing more than a rather inefficient employer. She had lain awake at night on more than one occasion wondering why his smile had the effect of making her heart leap, and why she was glad to be able to seek him out on the rare occasions she did not know what to do with a piece of correspondence. She had caught herself once or twice making up reasons to see him, and then castigated herself afterwards for her silliness. When he had proposed this trip to Deering, she told herself she had accepted because she wanted to talk over matters of the estate. But she knew better.

So they accomplished their journey in record time, Tom blowing the yard of tin to good purpose, each entirely unaware of the thoughts of the other.

Chapter Fourteen

"My dear, you are most welcome here," exclaimed his lordship's mother, when they arrived. "Although you will find it dreadfully flat. Apart from the last hunt, the only thing we plan at this time of the year is a dinner with neighborhood friends after Easter. No one fashionable at all! It will be very quiet. As you may know, my daughter and the grandchildren are presently in Vienna, so there will be no children for the rolling down the hill."

Amelia laughed. "In that case, it will suit me very well indeed. I'm familiar with the tradition of the rolling of colored eggs at Easter, but I assure you, I shall not miss it. I am hoping to do some hunting, if his lordship can mount me. But apart from that, I am concerned only with various estate affairs the agent has been in touch with me about. And I'm sure you can see already," indicating her rather worn driving cloak, "I'm not a fashionable person. I brought no evening clothes, so I hope I may be excused from any dinners, even with friends."

Lady Elizabeth Ailesbury had not been unaware of the state of Miss Moreton's cloak, but neither had she been unaware of the light in her son's eye as he had helped her down from the curricle. It was the first time he had brought home a woman of any sort, so fashionable or not, this one was not going to take her meals in her room.

"Nonsense," she said. "I'm sure we can find something for you to wear. We are much of a size, you and I."

It was true. Her ladyship was almost as tall as Amelia, and while no longer as slender as a girl, she still had a fine, upright figure. Amelia thanked her, privately vowing to stay as far away from friendly neighborhood dinners as she could. She would ride, do her work and that's all. She needed no more reasons for her heart to leap in that ridiculous manner.

But dinner the first evening set the pattern for the rest of the stay. Amelia protested in vain that she had not expected to dine *en famille*, but she was firmly overruled, both by the Earl and his mother. The maid who unpacked her suitcase carried the shocking word to her ladyship's dresser that Miss Moreton was entirely without evening attire. The dresser, scandalized, lost no time in informing her employer. Lady Elizabeth, saying she was aware one of Miss Moreton's trunks had unaccountably been left behind in London, directed her to carry two or three of her gowns to the secretary and to stay to help her. The dresser was inclined to be annoyed at this misuse of her talents, until it appeared that Miss Moreton didn't expect to use them. She could manage on her own and did not need her.

Watching her attempting to pin up her wild hair, the dresser's professional pride took over. She masterfully caught up Amelia's glorious tresses on top of her head and arranged them falling behind in natural ringlets. Then she helped her into the borrowed gown. In the end, she congratulated herself on the sight of Miss Moreton in the dark green silk shadow-stripe. It had never become her ladyship, as her dresser had told her often and again, and it was anyway a trifle too tight. Now she persuaded herself that lending it had been her idea all along. Amelia, not accustomed to placing too much importance on her appearance, hardly glanced in the mirror before descending, and was unaware of the picture she presented. As she walked into the sitting room, the Earl stood up, his eyebrows rising in unconscious appreciation. His mother saw it and congratulated herself just as her dresser had done. Amelia looked lovely.

For her secretarial functions she normally wore the plainest of dark colored dresses, most often with a demure white collar. Her hair was usually tied back simply, with pins making a vain attempt to control the escaping tendrils. Her employer had never seen her in an evening gown before. It was cut low and her elegant neck rose from a white bosom made all the more stunning by the deep green of the gown. Her fiery red ringlets tumbled in controlled abundance from their top-knot securely fixed by the professional hand of the dresser.

"Yes," said her ladyship with satisfaction. "I knew that gown would become you. It always made me look sallow. I can't imagine why I chose the color for myself, but on you, Miss Moreton, it is perfect. I wish you would keep it."

Amelia hardly knew what to answer, but her confused thanks were interrupted by his lordship leading her to the settee and offering her a glass of sherry. This she took gladly. She was accustomed to attending her parents' dinner parties from the earliest age and these were often a good deal more unconventional than this family dinner. She needed no Dutch courage to face company. But she had no experience at all of a heart that would not behave itself. Now she foresaw spending the evenings with the Earl and wondered how she could avoid them. She almost wished she suffered from headaches, so she might use them as an excuse.

Tonight they were only four at table. Her ladyship had a companion, a Miss Soames, whose main job seemed to be to fetch and carry forgotten fans, lost shawls and unaccountably mislaid books. When dinner was announced, the Earl led in his mother, the butler led Amelia in and a footman came behind with Miss Soames. The fact that the secretary had been placed above the companion spoke volumes.

The dining room was huge, with two fireplaces, both blazing. The spring evening was cool, but not cold enough to warrant such extravagance. In fact, at one point, the Earl asked a footman to crack open one of the windows.

"It's hot as blazes in here, Mama," he said. "I don't know how you can stand it."

"All very well for you men," retorted his mother. "You are wearing a shirt, a waistcoat and a coat. Not to mention a neckcloth. We women are forced to be practically naked on top. Don't you agree, Miss Moreton?"

Before she could answer, the Earl laughed, "But it is Miss Moreton who makes us practice economy! We are no longer permitted to have fires in the unoccupied rooms more than once a month, and only one of the fireplaces in the dining and sitting rooms at Ailesbury House may be lit at a time!"

Her ladyship turned shocked eyes upon Amelia, who was forced to defend herself.

"I have never said anyone should be cold! I have only tried to be more...," she was going to say reasonable, until she remembered that it was by her ladyship's order that all the fires had previously been lit. "More... careful with resources." Then, warming to her theme, "After all, one fireplace per room should be enough for a man living alone, especially if he is out most evenings. And his lordship knows that if company is expected, more fires will be lit."

The Earl laughed again, but his Mama protested, "But one never knows when one may desire to go into a different room. And I cannot abide a cold chamber." She shuddered.

"Of course," added Amelia quickly, "if... when you come to Ailesbury House, my lady, all the fires will be lit, as you previously desired."

"You see, Mama," said her incorrigible employer, "it's no use to argue with Miss Moreton. She has an answer for everything. And I'm sure the household is being run with such economy, we shall soon be able to buy a Dower House in London for you where you may have fires lit all day every day all year, even when you aren't there."

Now her ladyship was forced to laugh too. "But Ned, you silly boy. Why would I ever do such a thing?" Then the meaning of his words struck her, "Why do I need a Dower House?" She looked swiftly from the one to the other. "You aren't thinking of getting married?"

"No, Mama! Of course not!" cried the silly boy. "Don't you think you would have been the first to know? You are my favorite woman in all the world. The only person I've ever wanted to marry is you!" But even as he said it, the Earl knew this was no longer quite true.

Amelia joined in the general laughter and reflected how different it sounded when a fond mother called her boy Ned, compared with a... a... lightskirt (how vulgar she was being!) who only wanted rubies.

After dinner, they sat down to a few hands of whist. Amelia had played this too from her earliest days and remembered many a riotous evening with her own family. The thought brought a sudden tear to her eye and she found herself blinking.

"Are you quite well, Miss Moreton?" Amelia had not realized his lordship had been looking at her.

"Oh, yes, quite well, thank you. I just have a piece of... of dust in my eye, I think."

"Please, take this." He handed her a snowy white handkerchief with an ornate A embroidered in the corner. When he saw her looking at it with appreciation, he added, "Miss Soames is kind enough to embroider some for me every Christmas, beautiful work, isn't it?"

The Miss Soames in question blushed furiously and muttered something indistinct that might have been, "It's my pleasure to do it."

"There you go," said Amelia to herself. "Another silly woman in love with him."

The game of whist proved to be quite interesting. Amelia was paired with her ladyship, who proved to be an erratic player, capable of great brilliance but also reckless disregard. Miss Soames was timid and uninspiring but responded to the Earl's steady kindness and became more sure of herself. Miss Moreton was a very good player and the two ladies should have won. But by dint of bringing out the best in Miss Soames and never faltering himself, his lordship's was the partnership that triumphed.

"I never should have held back that ace," complained her ladyship. "I made sure I was going to have a major coup."

"No, you shouldn't, Mama," said her dutiful son. "You missed a good moment for what you thought was a better one. But if you had counted the cards, you would have known Miss Soames could trump it. Now, the winnings should all go to her, for a really brilliant play."

"Oh, this man is positively dangerous!" thought Amelia, looking at the companion's pink cheeks. She told herself she would not be his next victim.

Chapter Fifteen

The next morning after breakfast, at which only she and the Earl appeared, he invited Amelia to the stables to choose a horse. She swiftly changed into her tweed riding dress and reappeared, a small black jaunty hat with a turned-up brim pinned to her curls. The ensemble was worn but well fitted and his lordship thought few women could look as good as she did in an outfit worn for utility, not fashion. He too wore a well-used tweed jacket over close-fitting black britches and top boots. But no one would have mistaken him for anything but a gentleman. His coat fit him like a glove, his boots shone and his top hat gleamed in the morning sun.

The hunt was scheduled for two days' time. Walking to the stables, Amelia sniffed the air appreciatively.

"Hope the weather continues like this," she said, "perfect for hunting. Calm and cool. The scent should rise just right."

As they came into the stables, an odd sight met their eyes. Tom was seated on an enormous hunter whose back was so broad the boy's feet stuck out almost horizontally. He was leaning forward, stroking the horse's mane and whispering in its ear.

"Quite a sight, i'nt it, my lord?" said the head groom, coming up to the Earl who was viewing Tom with amazement. "As you know, Lucifer don't never let anyone new get near 'im, and when e's in one of 'is moods not anyone at all, saving yerself, my lord.

But I come in 'ere this mornin' an' that lad was a-sittin' up there a-talking to him calm as yer like. I ain't never seen nothin' like it."

"Stay back here, Miss Moreton," said the Earl, quietly. "As Graham here says, Lucifer is not usually so docile. I don't want to see you kicked, or worse." Then, turning to the groom, "Graham, show Miss Moreton something suitable for her to ride tomorrow."

He left her and walked calmly up to his hunter. The horse snickered in recognition, and he patted the long nose with his gloved hand.

"Well, Tom," he said, still in the same even tone, "you've made the acquaintance of Lucifer here."

"Yus, yer honor, I mean yer lordship," replied Tom. "Wunnerful 'orse 'e is. We bin 'avin a chat. 'E tole me 'is shoe is not on right. Yer better 'ave a look at it."

"Really? He told you that? Well, I'd better examine them. You keep talking to him and I'll do the honors. Tell him not to kick me."

"He won't kick yer while I'm 'ere," said Tom confidently.

The Earl smiled and bent to his task. He picked up the big horse's hooves one by one. They were not very clean, and sure enough, on the animal's hind right, the shoe was crooked. One of the nails had been dislodged.

He took a carrot from his pocket and gave it to the horse, then went to have a word with one of the under grooms, who snatched off his cap and held it, twisting it in his hands.

"When's the last time Lucifer's hooves were cleaned and checked?" he asked pleasantly.

"I... tried to do it yesterday when 'e come back from 'is gallop," said the young man, defensively. But he wouldn't let me near. I tole meself I'd come back later, but I... I forgot. I'm sorry, my lord."

"Do the horses frighten you?"

"No, sir." He looked up into the Earl's face. He wasn't angry. Encouraged, he said, "Well, yessir, they does, a bit."

"So why are you working in the stables?"

"Well, me dad, 'is rheumatics is so bad, he can't do much no more and me mum said I 'ad to get whatever was goin'. They needed a groom, and took me on."

"And what work would you prefer?"

The young man hesitated. "I like doin' the garden, sir. Not vegetables. The flowers. We don't 'ave many at 'ome, bein' as we need the space for veg, but I likes to see the blossoms. That I does. The gardens 'ere is wunnerful."

"Then you will transfer to gardening work. I'm not sure how that may be accomplished, but I know someone who does. What is your name?"

"Barnaby Wood, sir. Barny."

"Very well, Mr. Wood... Barny. I'll see to it."

And his lordship walked over to where he could see his secretary in conversation with the head groom. Mr. Barnaby Wood couldn't believe it not only had he not been summarily dismissed for not doing his job, but it looked like he might get to do what he really liked. He had never met his lordship before. Not many of the tenants had. He rarely did the rounds of his estate, even when he was there. But what a story Barny could tell them at home tonight. The man was a real champion! A corker!

By this time, Amelia had dismissed the first three horses proposed by the head groom as seeming too docile. He had, of course, tried to find something suitable for a lady. She was now standing next to a large brown horse who snorted and tossed his head at her when she approached. Just like the Earl, she walked up quietly, looking the horse straight in the eye, and produced a piece of apple from her pocket.

"He'll do, I think," she said to the groom. "But I won't know till I've ridden him, if you would please get him saddled."

"But Miss, he's not a lady's horse. He'll run away with you!" said the groom in alarm.

"I don't want a lady's horse, and if he runs away with me, I'll give you ten guineas," pronounced Amelia.

Seeing the Earl approaching, the groom tried to enlist his help. "Sir," he said, "Miss is insisting on riding Rightabout. 'E'll 'ave 'er off, for sure."

"Oh, I don't think so, Graham. Miss Moreton knows horses. Get someone to saddle him up. I need you to get Lucifer to the blacksmith's. His right hind shoe is loose. The boy who should have checked it yesterday was afraid to do it, not surprisingly, if it put him in a temper. I might hesitate to do it myself without help."

"That's Barny, my lord. Bloody useless 'e is. I'll send 'im away with a flea in 'is ear."

"No, Mr. Wood will be transferred to work in the flower gardens." He smiled at Amelia. "I've no idea how that may be done, but I'm sure you have."

"Miss Moreton is the one who brought us young Tom." he said, turning to the groom. "He's still in conversation with Lucifer. The horse told him about the shoe, apparently. He quite rightly passed the message on to me. Anyway, horses and young men," and older ones too, he thought but didn't say, "Miss Moreton knows how to deal with them. She may have whichever horse she wants. I don't doubt even Lucifer would obey her. Especially if Tom told him to. He told him not to kick me when I was examining his hooves, and he didn't. I'm now wondering whether I should leave the boy here instead of taking him back to London."

The head groom went off, shaking his head, wondering if his lordship was a trifle bosky, even though it was only ten in the morning.

In due course Rightabout, so named because that's where he sent any rider he did not care for, was saddled for Miss Moreton. Using the block, she mounted him and called for the stirrup to be shortened slightly. Then she settled herself and her long skirts. She clicked to the horse and he ambled out of the stables, the model of a well-behaved mount. She waited for the Earl to join her, which he did on another of his hunters, and they set out.

They left the gates of Deering House and headed up a path that wound gently to the top of a hill behind it. Rightabout tried unsuccessfully to dismount his rider by a series of bucks and sideways steps which caused her to brush up hard against bushes on the side of the path, followed by short bursts of speed that ended in abrupt stops. Amelia let him have his way until he had tried all his tricks and then spoke sternly to him.

"It's no good. I'm on here, stuck like glue. You may as well get used to it and not tire yourself out by this performance."

She patted his head and stroked his ears a few times. He remembered the piece of apple, and apparently decided that he'd met a match. She might give him another piece if he behaved. He settled down.

When they got to the top of the hill, a broad expanse lay before them. The riders looked at each other and by mutual understanding urged their horses into a fine long gallop. It was neck and neck all the way, and if his lordship won by a head, it was only because he knew the terrain better than she. They pulled up, panting, and slid off their mounts.

"You are a very fine horsewoman, Miss Moreton," said his lordship, as they stood surveying the view before them. "I've never met a better. In fact, you ride better than most men. I congratulate you!"

"It's because I was lucky enough to have a twin brother and everything he did, I did too. Our parents were both very keen on sport and made no distinction between us. If you tell a child she, or he, can't do something, he or she will not, of course, be able to do it. I never heard that in my childhood. As a consequence I can do most things a man can do. Where I fall sadly short, though, is in the feminine accomplishments. I can't sew, paint, play an instrument or flirt with a fan." She laughed. "My mother had no time for those things and neither do I!"

"You don't find not being able to flirt with a fan an impediment?" his lordship's eyes twinkled.

She smiled back. "No, it hasn't been an accomplishment I have thus far needed. I'm afraid I'm not very good at being a woman."

"I wouldn't say that," replied the Earl, with an odd note in his voice. Then he collected himself. "We should be getting back.

Mother likes lunch on the table at one, and we have to change, of course."

They had been walking the horses, to allow them to cool down, but now his lordship helped Amelia back onto Rightabout by simply taking her around the waist and swinging her up. His unexpected closeness and the ease with which he lifted her, no lightweight, made her heart leap and her breath catch in her throat. Luckily, his lordship immediately remounted and eased his horse into a canter back to the path down the hillside. Then they had to pay attention on the sloping stone-ridden path. There was no opportunity for further conversation.

Chapter Sixteen

Amelia had written to Mr. Bright, the land agent, requesting him to meet her that afternoon. She asked Earl to participate in the meeting, but after her surge of emotions when he had lifted her onto her horse, she was glad when he said he had arranged to spend the afternoon visiting old friends in the neighborhood. In fact, he had made no such arrangement, but, like Amelia, he was still thinking about their closeness that morning. He had acted without thinking in putting his hands to her waist, but he could still feel her supple body beneath her riding dress and her faint perfume remained in his nose.

So he had responded as neutrally as he could, "I'll come with you to say hello to Bright and tell him you stand in my place. He's a nice old fellow. He'll probably bring his son with him. He's been telling me for years his son's going to step into his shoes, but he doesn't ever seem ready to take them off! By the way, would you mention to Bright about transferring young Barnaby from the stables to the flower gardens? He's no use as a groom. I trust he'll do better there. At least the roses don't kick!"

Mr. Bright Senior proved to be a man who was used to being listened to. He was above average height but now bent and using a cane. He had a full head of shocking white hair and his eyes were a piercing blue. He had a way of thrusting his chin towards the person he was talking to. It was rather disconcerting and Amelia could see that this characteristic, together with his forceful way of talking, must have always made him appear formidable. In her view, however, it was due to the fact he was and probably always had been myopic. This was proven when he asked his son, the junior Bright, to tell him the time, explaining that his eyes were giving him even more trouble nowadays.

Amelia told him his lordship's wish to transfer young Mr. Wood from a job he was no good at to one he preferred. He shook his head and said he didn't know what the world was coming to when youngsters thought they could pick and choose, but when she refused to be drawn into a discussion, harrumphed his acceptance. She then brought up the topic of the numerous repairs repeated from year to year and expounded on her theory that though expensive, if complete and proper renovations were done once, they would be cheaper in the long run. Bright Junior turned a grateful gaze upon her and said at once, "That's what I'm always telling him, but…." He got no further.

"Now you be keeping your thoughts to yourself, my boy," intervened his father. "What we've got here on this estate was good enough for my father and his father before him, and it's good enough for you. Aye, and your son too, if you can get on with it and make one! What am I to do with a tribe of grand-daughters?"

The "boy" in question blushed. He had to be at least 35. Like his father, he was above average height but of a sandy complexion with pale blue eyes and a more amenable countenance. He had none of his father's jutting ferocity. He must take after his mother.

"But, Mr. Bright, have you ever asked his lordship what his feelings were? I think I know him well enough to say that he would not begrudge money being spent to improve the long-term efficiency of the estate and the comfort of his tenants."

"No Miss Moreton, I have not, and such is not my intention. We shall do what we've always done – make do and mend. I'm not one to spend his blunt where it's not needed."

"I'm sure our employer is very grateful for your careful husbandry, Mr. Bright, and I shall be sure to tell him what you say. Now, if you please, I should like to see the cottages subject to spring flooding down by the river," responded Amelia pleasantly, but with no sign she was about to change her mind.

"I don't know why you want to go down there, Miss." said the old man. "Nasty smelly places they are."

"Oh, it interests me to see in the flesh, as it were, what I've only seen on paper," said Amelia, firmly. Privately she thought that if, indeed, they were nasty smelly places, she would definitely have something done about it, and soon. This might be her only chance to help the poor people living there.

She set off in a gig with Bright *père et fils* and after about a three-mile drive came to a row of sad-looking cottages set a little back from the banks of a fairly wide river, shining now in the spring sunshine. But it was obvious that it had recently flooded. The ground between the river and the front of the cottages was soft and muddy. It was also, as Mr. Bright had said, very odorous.

"I should like to go inside one or two of the cottages," announced Amelia.

"But Miss, we can't drive up to them," said Bright Junior. "The gig will get stuck. And if you walk, you'll sink up to your knees."

"People must be able to get to their homes even when there's deep mud in front," insisted Amelia. "There must be way to get round to the back. A lane or something. Turn the gig around."

Bright Senior grumbled about the waste of time, but acquiesced. They finally found a lane, little more than a footpath, that led to the somewhat higher ground at the back of the cottages. Coming upon the dwellings from that angle, the full misery of the tenants' living conditions was revealed. They had obviously been forced to move what they could outside behind the cottages. The back yards were a jumble of chairs, tables and bedframes. Here and there lean-to's had been fashioned, covered with straw, sticks, bits of old clothing, in short, anything that would make a shelter. Girls were crouched over open fires, stirring the contents of black pots placed on stones in the center. Barefoot children, their legs covered in mud up to the thighs, were climbing over the rickety piles of furniture. Bare-bottomed infants crawled on the scrubby grass, urinating or defecating wherever they found themselves. Mothers looked around hopelessly, their skirts tucked up into the waistband of their filthy aprons, their petticoats inches deep in mud, dirt-encrusted wooden pattens on their feet.

"But this is abominable!" exclaimed Amelia. "I'm sure his lordship has no idea his tenants are living like this! Has he ever seen it?"

"I don't rightly know," replied Bright Senior, a little sullenly. "Of course, it's not always like this. A bit of sun and it all dries up. They move back inside."

"And if it rains? If we have a wet spring? What then? We leave our people to live in the open? Even savages have huts! This cannot be allowed to continue."

Not waiting for a reply, Amelia sprang down from the gig and marched to the closest cottage, oblivious of the soft earth staining her boots and the brambles tearing at her clothing. She pushed open the gate and the fetid odor of the privy immediately met her nose. She held her breath and walked fearlessly forward. As she did so, all activity in the yard ceased. Even the baby stopped crawling in the muddy grass. A woman whose age Amelia could not begin to guess stared at her as if she were a heavenly apparition.

"Good afternoon," said Amelia with a smile. "I am his lordship's secretary. He wishes to help you. May I look inside your home? I need to see what may be done."

"Lord love you, Ma'am," said the woman. "There ain't nothing can be done 'cept you tell that river not to rise. Same thing every March. 'E comes in the front door, we goes out the back. But please yerself. 'Ave a look inside if yer likes."

Amelia pushed open the wooden door and stepped into the cottage. It was all one room, with a deep fireplace on one side. The walls were obviously very old wattle and daub, patched with handfuls of straw or bits of wood. High water marks stained the walls about a foot from the floor at the front of the cottage, lower as it moved towards the back. The roof thatch, also much patched, was held up by ancient rafters over which the bed mattress and household linen were presently festooned. The floor itself was mud, liquid mud. The whole place stank: rot, mildew and human waste. She had no doubt that if she visited the rest of the cottages in the row, she would find the same thing.

Amelia mentally counted the children she had seen in the yard outside. There had been two girls, a young lad and a baby. If there were older boys, they would be in the fields with their father. There were probably at least seven people living in this one room, with one bed and the bits and pieces of furniture she had seen outside. Every year they would be forced to move all their belongings into the back yard, hope it didn't rain, and wait for the water in their home to go down. Well, she said to herself. No more.

The solution was obvious. The cottages should be torn down and moved back onto the higher ground. They should have been rebuilt years ago in any case. These places looked hundreds of years old! This was the nineteenth century, not the middle ages! A flood wall would be built along the river, and the area between the houses and the flood wall sowed with tall grass to absorb any overflow.

"Mr. Bright," she said pleasantly to the senior agent on the way back to Deering House, "I know you will approve of my bringing his lordship back here tomorrow to show him the conditions his tenants are living in. He will be glad you have the problem in hand. I'm sure you must often have considered the idea of building new cottages back about fifty feet from their present location, but have been hesitant to put the cost of such a project to him. But when he sees these conditions I am convinced he will agree with you that it is the only solution." She smiled encouragingly at him.

"But I never...," he blustered.

"Of course," she intervened quickly, "you would never put such an idea to him without good reason. The cost of such a venture, together, of course, with building a flood wall, could only be suggested by a loyal and faithful servant such as yourself. In matters such as these, he places all his trust in you and your family." She smiled at Bright the younger, who was looking at her with admiration.

"Well, I suppose...."

"Yes, you do well to suppose that the work could be carried out over two years. The cottages may be torn down and rebuilt this year and the flood wall next year. But I'm inclined to think his lordship will be of the mind of in for a penny, in for a pound, as the saying goes. I can tell you that in his London home he has introduced every modern convenience as soon as it has become available. He is a great believer in progress."

In this Miss Moreton spoke far from the truth. The indolent Earl would not know a modern convenience unless he sat upon it, but this description of him was far more likely to bear the fruit she was after.

"But you may suggest whatever you think best, of course. You are the expert here."

This view so accorded with his own idea of himself that Mr. Bright père found himself nodding in agreement with this startling young woman.

"Well, of course," he said finally, "Them cottages is very old and no doubt there's better could be built, and away from that damn…, excuse me Miss…, from that river. What d'you say, Robbie?" He turned to his son.

Robbie had just had a lesson in diplomacy that would serve him well the rest of his life. He used it now.

"You're quite right father. As you've said oft and again, something needs to be done, and there's none better than you to do it."

Since his father had been as obstinate as a mule his whole life, his son was embroidering freely here, but the new approach bore fruit.

"'Tis as you say, my boy. We'll talk to 'is lordship tomorrow and being as he's a modern man, he'll listen to reason."

"Aye, and I remember you told me about those new cottages down Ditchling way. Very nice you said they was. If Ditchling can do it, we can do it better!"

In fact, Bright Senior had loudly criticized the Ditchling landlord for his profligacy, but that was forgotten as father and son beguiled the return journey in a technical discussion about trusses, joists, struts and other terms that were a mystery to Amelia.

The following morning, she and the Earl went back to the river cottages, where they met Bright and Son. When the Earl saw the dreadful conditions his tenants were forced to endure, his eyes narrowed and he went quite white about the lips. In a voice she had never heard him use, he demanded to know why he hadn't been informed of this before.

"Sir," she said, before either of the Brights had a chance to explain, "No blame attaches to Mr. Bright and his son. Indeed," and here she again embroidered the truth, "they have often discussed permanent solutions. But they thought to protect your pocket. And you must know, what you are seeing here is the situation at its worst. With a little sunshine, it will all dry up." She consciously repeated the agent's words to her the day before.

"Even dry, the inside of those hovels can only be a disgrace," said his lordship. "I can't imagine why things have been allowed to deteriorate in this way."

But, of course, he could imagine why. It was because he had never troubled himself to know. His father had left everything to Bright's management, and he had followed suit. He suddenly realized what a poor landlord he had been.

"No, no," he said, as the agent began to embark upon an explanation, "it is entirely my responsibility and I must shoulder the blame. I have been remiss in my duties as a landlord, and I'm very sorry for it. But these cottages are to be replaced as soon as may be, and I shall expect a detailed report on the conditions of the living accommodations of all my tenants very shortly."

"And the flood wall?" said Amelia in a low voice.

"And a flood wall is to be constructed before the winter. I believe it has been suggested tall grass be sown between the river and the houses. See to it, Bright."

The Earl and his secretary drove off. He was very quiet until Amelia suggested they examine the state of the bridge over the river. She had seen from the accounts that it was repaired every year. Perhaps that, too, needed replacement. But when they arrived at it, she saw it was a nice old arched stone bridge, built where the river was narrowest.

"My God," said his lordship. "I've ridden over this bridge a thousand times in my life and never thought to question how it stays up. I see now the weight is distributed to the stone supports at each end. The water must rise up during the spring flood, and they show evidence of repair, but it all looks sturdy enough. Shall we drive over it? I daresay you add swimming to your list of physical accomplishments!"

"Yes, but I don't fancy a dunking," she laughed.

In the event, the drive over and back was perfectly safe and they left the bridge standing just as it had stood in everyone's memory, and longer.

As they trotted easily along, however, the Earl said suddenly, "I'm very grateful to you, Miss Moreton, for making me see where my management of the estate has been at fault. I'm ashamed to admit how little thought I've given to it. I do not mean to blame my father, for the choice has been my own, but he never seemed to pay it much attention, and neither have I."

"I must say, my initial interest was purely financial. When I looked at the accounts of the last few years, I saw that money was being spent on the same things year after year: the thatch for the roofs, the daub for the walls, pieces of timber to replace rotting ones. I simply thought it must be cheaper to repair properly once and for all. But when I saw the reality of it, I realized people's lives were involved. Imagine returning after a day working in the fields and not having a dry place to sit, or to sleep in. It is our duty to make sure those who work for us have the means to live good and upright lives. Squalor begets squalor, both physical and mental."

Amelia realized she was almost preaching and halted, with a little laugh. "I'm sorry, my lord. I should not go on so."

"It's a pity there are no women in politics," responded the Earl smiling. "You would be admirable in the House!"

His comment reminded her unpleasantly of what she would soon be forcing him to do, and she lapsed into a guilty silence for the rest of the trip.

Chapter Seventeen

Miss Moreton appeared for breakfast before dawn the next morning and found her employer already addressing a plate of ham and eggs. He stood and told her that on hunt mornings the staff put out dishes on the sideboard, and she should please help herself. Knowing they would not eat again for several hours, she too ate a hearty meal and then walked with him to the stables where Rightabout and Lucifer had been saddled.

They were both wearing the traditional red hunting jackets and white neck cloth. Amelia's coat was cut into the waist, flaring out over a long black wool skirt. The Earl's, buttoned high on the chest, fit without a wrinkle across his broad shoulders and hung almost straight to the top of his muscular thighs. He wore close-fitting white trousers, a tall black hat and black riding boots that shone, even in the dark of the pre-dawn morning. Amelia had on the same little black hat with the turned-up brim. She had braided her hair down her back in an attempt to keep it together for the hunt, but curls were already escaping from the sides. They gleamed in the early light.

The meet was at the local squire's, where the local, predominantly male, hunting population was beginning to gather. Amelia saw only one other woman and made her way to her side. Under these conditions, she thought the lack of formal introduction was forgivable. The lady turned out to be Brenda Dobbs, sister of the widowed squire, a spinster of about forty with a mannish demeanor and gruff voice. However, she was very friendly and undertook to seek Amelia out when they should return, to show her where the facilities might be found inside the house. Like Amelia, she was looking forward to a day's hunting and said she hoped for a good run.

As the sun rose, they were offered a stirrup-cup of brandy which both ladies took, Amelia because the morning was cool and she was getting chilled waiting, Brenda because she drank brandy, she said, like mother's milk. After a few more minutes, the group moved out of the yard and into the open. The master signaled for the hounds to move off and draw the covert. Their white tails could be seen waving above the gorse. Then a baying indicated a fox had been scented. The horn sounded and to the call of Tally-ho, they were off, following the hounds. Then View-halloo, the fox broke cover and ran into the open. Amelia and Brenda were among the first group, or field. They were both experienced riders and would take the straightest course: jumping over gates, hedges or other obstacles. Behind them came the second field, more sedate riders who enjoyed the sociability of being with friends and would go around rather than over obstacles. Lastly there were a few, mostly young village lads, who liked to run behind and witness the fun.

The fox led them a merry dance. He broke the scent by running along the top of walls. He led them miles up one side of a stream and then, where it was narrowest, crossed it so the hounds lost the scent and had to be whipped-in. He was then seen by the lads in the third field as he doubled back the way he had come. Amelia enjoyed herself enormously, not caring whether the fox was caught, in fact, rather wishing he wouldn't be, as he seemed so clever. Rightabout had by now recognized who was master and did anything she wanted. They sailed over five-bar gates, skimmed the tops of hedges and flew over stiles. Her braid sailed out behind her, becoming increasingly loose, so that her wild curls ran riot all round her face.

When Master Reynard did his doubling back act and they had to turn around, Amelia found herself for the first time next to her employer. He looked at her glowing face and disheveled coiffure.

"It's easy to see you are enjoying yourself," he said with a laugh. "Every time I look up I see you way ahead, your hair streaking out behind you like the fox's brush. Be careful! Someone might cut it off and take it home for a trophy!"

"Oh, I almost wish they would!" she exclaimed, making ineffective motions to tuck it under her hat. "It's the bane of my life!"

"Don't say so," answered his lordship. "It's glorious. I can't imagine you without it. And," he said, looking over his shoulder back at her, "it means you can never get lost. You can be seen from miles away! Race you to the bottom of the stream!"

He urged Lucifer into a gallop.

"Wait, you cheat! You began before me!" cried Amelia. She lay low over Rightabout's neck and pushed him forward with her heel and her voice. The Earl made the mistake of looking back to see where she was, and in that instant, she flew by him and never lost the lead again. Lucifer was bigger and stronger, but his lordship was much heavier. Rightabout could have carried a man at least three stone heavier than Amelia. When they drew up at the bottom where the fox had disappeared, both horses and riders were panting. The riders slid off.

"You cheated, you know you did!" gasped Amelia.

"Yes, and much good it did me," he replied with a laugh. "But I shall have my revenge one day, you see if I don't!"

"Don't count on it," she retorted. "I always beat my brother. Like you, he's too much of a gentleman and always looks back to see if I've come to grief. I never looked back to see how you were doing, perhaps you noticed!"

"No, I didn't!" He laughed again. "Oh, the injustice of it! I lost because I'm a gentleman!"

"And I won because I'm not!" said Amelia, her head in the air.

And they companionably walked their beasts to where the master was assembling the hounds and the other hunters.

"Reynard's gone to earth," he said. "We could set the terriers down the den, if we could find it, but he's a sly one and chances are we'd be wasting our time." He looked up at the sky. "Looks like it's coming on to rain, too, so I'm calling it a day. Don't know about you chaps—and ladies," with a quick smile at Amelia and Brenda, "but I'm for breakfast."

"God knows why it's called breakfast," said Brenda in her gruff way, as they trotted back to the Grange, "no matter what time you eat it. It must be past two."

After handing the horses over to the waiting grooms, Amelia followed the other lady into the house where she was shown a bedchamber for her use. She removed her hat and attempted to bring some order to her hair. She had no brush, so she simply undid the braid, ran her fingers through her curls and replaited it. It was not altogether successful: curls immediately sprang from the sides and over her brow. But it would have to do. She washed her hands and face and with no further thought to her appearance, went back downstairs.

So that the mud from boots and the débris from jackets would not ruin the host's dining room, by tradition the hunt breakfast was served on trestle tables set up in the hall. The men stood around in groups, most with tankards in their hands, waiting for their hostess to arrive and take her place. In spite of her disheveled coiffure, or perhaps because of it, all the male eyes turned towards Amelia as she came down the stairs, her hat and whip in her hands. Her abundant fiery curls and the rich red of her hunting jacket seemed to focus all the light in the room on her, and the nipped-in waist and full skirt enhanced her figure.

"Good God, who's that?" muttered one of the hunters who had not seen Amelia take off in the first line.

"Came with Ned Woodbridge, lucky fellow. She's staying up at the House apparently. Must have brought her home to meet Mama."

"Are we to wish him happy?"

"Haven't heard anything."

"Interesting. So there may still be a chance for us lesser mortals. Excuse me, my friend, but destiny beckons."

He bowed slightly and walked straight over to Amelia. He bowed again, not so slightly this time and said, "Rupert Branford, at your service, Ma'am. I apologize for dashin' up to you like this, no introduction and all. But who is there to introduce us? Do you know any of these fellows?" he looked vaguely around.

"No!" laughed Amelia, "I'm Amelia Moreton." She briefly took his hand. "I know no one except my employer and the hostess, and I only met her today."

"Your employer?" Mr. Branford could not keep the astonishment from his voice.

"Yes, Earl of Ailesbury. I'm his secretary."

"Secretary?" He just stopped himself from saying, "Is that what they're calling it in London these days?"

"Yes, his previous one went abroad and I took the position." Amelia knew perfectly well what he was thinking and adopted a repressive tone. "I came with his lordship because I wanted to see for myself the condition of some of the cottages on the estate. He is undertaking a series of renovations."

"Ned Woodbridge? Renovations?" Mr. Branford's astonishment grew. "I'm surprised to hear he knows he has cottages."

"You wrong him, sir," answered Miss Moreton. "He is well aware of what is required."

At that moment, the hostess came down the stairs. She stopped a few steps from the bottom and said loudly in her gruff voice, "Don't stand on ceremony! We're all friends here. No names, no drill. Just sit anywhere."

There was a shuffling of feet but no one sat until she had plumped herself down at the head of the table. Amelia found herself propelled forward by Mr. Branford. Her only savior might have been the Earl, but he was engaged in conversation at the other end of the room, so she not very willingly found herself seated between Branford and another man whom he introduced. "Tony Smithers. Friend of mine. Tony, this is Miss Moreton. Secretary to Ned Woodbridge." He put a slight emphasis on the word.

Mr. Smithers' eyes opened wide and his friend carried on, "Yes, she's here looking at cottages. Ned's doing some renovations, it seems."

"Renovations? His secretary eh? Oh, er, well, jolly good." Mr. Smithers hardly knew what to say. Then he remembered his upbringing. "And how did you enjoy the hunt, Miss Moreton?"

This gave all of them the opening they needed for a discussion on much firmer ground. It soon became clear to the two men that Amelia was an avid fox hunter and could hold her own as they told anecdotes each more outlandish than the last. As might be expected, a number of these were very humorous. The Earl, looking down the table to see where Amelia was sitting, saw her laughing heartily with her companions. He had planned to sit next to her himself but had been waylaid at the last minute by a neighboring landowner.

The "breakfast" was long and copious, as befits a crowd of hungry men after a hunt. It wasn't long before his lordship heard the word *secretary* murmured around the table and realized that speculation about him and Miss Moreton was rife. While continuing to participate mechanically in the conversations on either side of him, he asked himself exactly what direction their relationship was heading in. Was he thinking of her as a wife? Would she even accept him? He had no satisfactory answer. In the end, he was glad he had not sat with her, and when the meal was over made no attempt to speak to her until it was time to ride home.

It was nearly five before the Earl and Miss Moreton arrived back at Deering House. During the ride back they exchanged only superficial remarks on the day. The closeness they had both felt after their race was replaced by reticence. Each was aware of the gossip, and they both had the sense that during the hunt they had crossed some sort of Rubicon. But neither was by any means sure what lay on the other side.

Chapter Eighteen

Dinner that night was again a quiet affair. Guests had been invited for the day after Easter, but until then, according to the tradition of the house, they were to observe a Lenten simplicity. Having eaten a very substantial "breakfast", Amelia was glad of it. She was glad too when she observed that the card table had been put away, her hostess explaining that it was not considered seemly to play cards during the days leading up to Easter. The Earl made his apologies very soon after dinner, saying vaguely he had something to do. In fact, he went into the billiard room and smoked a thoughtful cigar.

His mother began a not-so-subtle interrogation of the girl she had at first thought might be her future daughter-in law. But, she had to admit, since they had been there she could discern no particular closeness between Miss Moreton and her son. They laughed together, it was true, but she never saw them with their heads bent close, or sharing a secret glance. Still, perhaps the lady had been strictly brought up and would have considered such behavior unacceptable. But it seemed doubtful. For one thing, there was that mass of red hair, generally not indicative of a retiring nature. And listening to her hearty laugh when something amused her, Amelia most certainly did not display the characteristics of a shy damsel.

However, as she talked to Miss Moreton, her ladyship became convinced of two things. First, she was not in love with her son, and secondly, even if she were, she would be entirely unsuitable as his wife. What she didn't realize was that Amelia was perfectly aware of the nature of the interrogation and did not want to give her ladyship any straw with which to make bricks. So she deliberately gave the impression she regarded the Earl as nothing more than her employer. Without actually saying so, she conveyed the idea she considered him lacking in depth, a fashionable fribble, no more. No mother likes to hear a woman criticize her son for exactly the shortcomings she herself has blamed him for, and Lady Elizabeth was not best pleased.

And if this did not make her an unsuitable partner, Miss Moreton's entire lack of feminine accomplishments did. Here again, Amelia deliberately overemphasized the unconventional nature of her upbringing, her love of sport and her dislike of domesticity. She airily disclaimed any predilection for the feminine arts. But she liked card games and was quite a good billiard player. Her ladyship shuddered. A new Lady Ailesbury would have to take her place amongst the hostesses of the ton. An ability at billiards would hardly recommend her. To be unable to give directions for balls or even know how to dress suitably would be serious drawbacks. Her ladyship now began to see Amelia as a woman impatient of convention who deliberately flouted the norms of society. The admiration of her unexpected beauty revealed by the borrowed gown was replaced by the critical reflection that the young woman had not even had the sense to bring anything to wear to dinner.

"She won't do, you know," said her ladyship to her son a day or so later, while he was accompanying her on a walk around the garden.

"Who won't do what?" answered the Earl, playing for time. He knew exactly what his mother was talking about.

"Miss Moreton. She would not make a good wife for you."

"Good Lord, Mama! Whatever put that into your head? Miss Moreton is my secretary. That is all."

"I'm glad to hear it. I thought at first there might be something more."

"Well, there's not. And I'm sure Miss Moreton has no such intentions towards me."

"No, she doesn't," said his mother. "She thinks you a fashionable fribble. And I did not get the sense even rank and fortune would overcome her feelings."

"So I am!" laughed his lordship, though the words wounded him more than he would have thought possible.

With neither of them willing to acknowledge their deepest feelings, and both aware of her ladyship's opinion, contact between his lordship and his secretary over the next few days was necessarily strained. The dinner with friends on Easter Monday was a relief, for it brought more company to Deering House. Rupert Branford and Tony Smithers were invited and eagerly pursued their acquaintance with Amelia. Her ladyship had deliberately placed them on either side of her at table, at a distance from her son, and Miss Moreton demonstrated her best company manners by keeping them entertained with lively conversation.

The net result was that for the days remaining after the Easter holiday, Amelia received invitations to ride out with one or the other every day. That pleased her, for it gave her an opportunity to see other parts of the estate and surrounding country, and kept her from the orbit of her employer. If the young men thought she was going for their sake, she never disabused them.

She was always charming company but treated them rather as she treated her brother. When the time came for her to leave, they were both inclined to fancy themselves in love, but neither of them could for a minute deceive himself that he had captured her heart.

There were now only two weeks to the date of the Maiden Speech. Amelia had successfully put it out of her head while she was dealing with the affairs of Deering estate, but back in London, she was painfully conscious of the day drawing ever nearer when she would have to tell her employer what she had done. She was glad he never seemed to be at home. She would hear his voice in the hall as he left, and she would be gone before he returned. She couldn't have guessed that he was deliberately staying away, or that, after returning from wherever it had been, he couldn't stop himself from going into her office on some pretext just to breathe in the lingering scent of her.

The one thing that distracted her from the approaching trial was her brother. He was looking quite unlike his normal self. His sunny disposition had been replaced by a haunted look. When she asked him what the matter was, he shrugged, saying he was just a little tired. He hadn't been sleeping well. In fact he was still staying out late and sleeping until all hours of the day.

"If you'd go to bed at a reasonable hour and get up at one, you'd feel a lot better," she admonished him, sounding more like his mother than his sister. "Your night time extravagances don't seem to bring you much satisfaction, in any case."

He muttered something non-committal and left her.

This would have worried her more, but Amelia found herself thinking about the speech she was going to have to compose for his lordship. She knew she had to strike the right note for a man well known to his peers. It couldn't be too serious, at least in the beginning, for that was unlike him. On the other hand, there was no avoiding the seriousness of the subject. Luckily, she knew it must be quite short, not more than ten minutes. But the beauty of it was that tradition held no one could leave during a Maiden Speech, so as long as a reasonable complement of peers was in the House, he would be sure of a good audience.

After chewing the end of her pen thoughtfully for a while, she began:

> *You are no doubt astonished to see me here before you, my lords, a man known as the least impassioned amongst you, unless it be on the correct temperature to serve a bottle of Château d'Yquem or the exact length of a gentleman's coat. (Pause for laughter) But here I am.*

> *This is because I was jolted out of my normal complacency by a discovery I made recently. I am talking about the shocking conditions pertaining inside the factories and manufactories of our great land. Those of you who live in the northern counties may be familiar with them. But for those who are not, you need look no further than the City of London, where a cotton mill down on the Thames will open your eyes. The conditions there were brought home to me recently by a chance encounter.*

She felt that a real story would hold the attention of the audience as nothing else would, so the speech went on to tell the story of Tom, with the Earl acting in her place. She described the discovery of the starving Tom on the streets of Mayfair and the return to his place of employment. She described in detail what she had seen and how Tom had effectively been sold like a slave to the overseer of the mill.

Then came a review of the 1809 Factory Act. As they no doubt knew, this had been aimed specifically at the conditions relating to apprentices. It required that factories be properly ventilated, that apprentices be provided with clothing and have access to basic hygiene. They had to receive an elementary education and attend a religious service at least once a month. Their working hours were limited to no more than twelve hours a day. They were not to work at night. But, the speech went on to emphasize, the Act did not attempt to address the working conditions of children who were not apprentices. There were no limits to specify the terms by which a person might hire workers who were not apprenticed: men, women and so-called free children. As a consequence, women and children could be employed in those appalling conditions. That, he said, is what he now wished to see addressed by the House. He was proposing the Act be revisited and expanded.

Then she concluded in a flight of oratory that she hoped his lordship would not refuse to utter:

My lords, if anyone had told me what I would
observe that day at a cotton mill in the East End,
here in London, in the heart of a city that is the finest
in the world, I would not have believed it. Neither
would I have believed that a member of this House
could be complicit in it, for one of our number is the
owner of this purgatory.

I could have thought myself in some far flung,
uncivilized part of this earth, the atmosphere as hot
and fetid as any jungle. Instead of curling tendrils to

catch the voyager unaware, the air was thick with white fibers that just as surely caught the throat; instead of the creatures that creep in the ooze and sludge, children were sliding on their bellies like snakes beneath the monstrous machine; instead of natives collecting wondrous fruit to feed their families, women were feeding the monstrous machine with matted balls for it to spew and spin into threads in order to clothe a ravening public.

Go yourselves, my lords, go and see. Like me, you will come back to this chamber determined to propose a new Act. A better Act, an Act that will protect the children of this land, both apprenticed and free, an Act that will enable them to grow up in health and security and make them bless forever the names of the men who proposed it.

Amelia made a fair copy of the whole speech and put it in her drawer.

The next week went crawlingly by. The speech lay in the drawer like some sort of incubus that she imagined might leap forth at any minute and smother her. Amelia did her work but found herself needing to stand up and walk around, go outside, anything to dissipate her nervous energy.

The Maiden Speech was to be given on Thursday, 13th April. On the Monday before, as was usual, Miss Moreton met with his lordship to go over his engagements for the upcoming week. Monday to Wednesday were quickly dealt with, but when she got to Thursday, she hesitated.

"My lord," she said, forcing herself to speak with her head up, "I fear you will not be happy with what I have to tell you. I have arranged for you to give your Maiden Speech in the House of Lords on Thursday at 11 o'clock."

He had been fiddling idly with a pen on his desk, looking into the distance, thinking about their ride to the top of the hill at Deering, and their race during the hunt. He replied with a laugh, "Oh very well, Miss Moreton. You caught me. I own I was daydreaming. I promise I shall pay attention. What am I to do on Thursday?"

"Give your Maiden Speech in the House of Lords."

"You can stop funning. I told you, you have my attention."

"I'm not funning, my lord," she replied, then added with a sort of desperation, "it was all because of Tom, you see."

"Tom? What's Tom got to do with it?"

The boy had, in the end, come back with them to London. Amelia had been with the Earl when it was suggested he might like to stay and work in the stables at Deering.

He hesitated for a moment but then said, "No yer hon... my lord. I want to come back to Lunnon. To be with Miss Moreton, y'see. I want to be where she is."

Amelia was touched. "Are you sure, Tom?" she asked. "I can come and see you, you know." Although after the Maiden Speech affair, she wondered if she would still have a job.

"Nah, I'd miss Lunnon anyways. It's too noisy 'ere in the country."

"Too noisy?"

"Yus. All them birds chirping fit to bust in the mornin' and the cocks crowin'. It's much more peaceful-like in Lunnon."

His lordship had laughed. "Very well, as you like. Come back to the quiet of the London streets with the hackneys rattling over the stones, the Watch calling the hours, parties of people hailing each other in the middle of the night."

"Yus, my lord. That's what I calls quiet. S'pose I'm used to it."

So here the lad was, in Albemarle Street, charming the maids by carrying their coal skuttles and pails, wheedling the cook to give him extra food, and when he wasn't in the stables talking to the horses, always keeping an eye out for Miss Moreton. By some alchemy, he knew when she was in the house and always contrived to meet her in the hall. When she left, he invariably met her on the pavement and walked with her to the end of the street.

"Yes, Tom. It was meeting him that began it all," she now replied.

She had never explained how she had discovered the boy begging in the street. All her employer knew was that he had been the new Boots. Now she told him the whole story and explained about her visit to the dreadful factory. It had convinced her that something had to be done. New legislation was absolutely necessary. She had written a speech. All he had to do was deliver it.

There was complete silence when she finished the end of her recitation. Then his lordship spoke, in a cold, calm voice she had only heard once before, when he saw the appalling conditions of his tenants at Deering.

"Let me understand this," he said. "You were horrified by what you saw. You decided, without consulting me, that I should be the agent by which change might be made. You somehow had my name put on the Parliamentary Calendar. Knowing that a colleague in the House is the owner of this enterprise, you wish me to expose it. You have been gracious enough even to write my speech. No doubt if you could, you would deliver it for me!"

"Yes," my lord," she said, earnestly. "I would. As it is, all you have to do is read it. Then I'll write to someone on your behalf and get them to propose a Bill. You won't have to do anything."

"And you think that's the kind of person I am?" said the Earl very angry now. He stood up and walked around the room with agitated steps. "I give my Maiden Speech at a time you have arranged. I read words you have written. I sign a letter you compose. I put in an appearance in the House when you tell me I must. Otherwise I carry on in my, what did my mother say you called it? Yes, my frippery way."

He didn't know if he was angriest because she'd put him in this position or because she so obviously thought he was incapable of independent thought or action.

"I think you'd better go now, Miss Moreton," he said at last. "You've done enough for today."

"But what about your engagements for the rest of the week?" faltered Amelia. "There's Lady Brough's ridotto on Friday and there's the Ranelagh spring ball on Saturday… I've ordered…."

"Just put the list down there. I can read. I am capable of independent thought, however much you may think the opposite!"

"Yes, my lord," she said, forlornly and walked to the door. "I'm sorry," she said, turning to look at him. "I see now that I should not have done what I did. But," she could not stop herself from adding, "the speech is in my desk drawer, should you want to look at it." And she quietly opened the door and left.

Chapter Nineteen

The Earl was so angry, he slammed out of the house and walked to his Club, where he proceeded to drink and play cards with unusual recklessness. He sat down to dine on the stodgy nursery food Gentlemen's Clubs invariably saw fit to serve their customers. Then, when he saw it, he regretted not going home for the much better meal Monsieur Antoine would undoubtedly have prepared. This made him angry all over again. He left the unappetizing fare on the plate, complaining loudly that no one in their right mind would eat a morsel of this God forsaken dog food. Then he decided to go home.

He had come on foot, but since it had begun to rain, all available hacks seemed to mysteriously disappear. He was too impatient to send for and then wait for his own vehicle, so he set forth to walk back to Albemarle Street. Within a few minutes he was drenched. He arrived home wet, hungry and in a foul temper. By then, the chef had retired to his own quarters with his second bottle of wine of the day and was in no condition to make his lordship's dinner. The sous-chef had her day off, so, as Bullock hesitatingly informed him, there was no dinner to offer him. Would he care for some of the bread and cheese the staff had had for their supper? No, he would not. He would go to bed, but by God, he'd better be served a decent breakfast or the whole lot of them would be looking for alternative employment.

The unexpected result of this unusual behavior was that when Bullock reported to Monsieur Antoine what his lordship had said, he was frightened into reducing his wine consumption. For a while the depredations to the Earl's cellar were significantly less. Not surprisingly, the chef outdid himself the following morning. A cheese soufflé was placed in the oven the minute his lordship's descent from his chamber was announced by a footman, placed on special watch for the purpose. It arrived, fluffy and fragrant at the table, just as the Earl, his head feeling as if it were bound in iron bands, had finished his second cup of coffee. A few minutes later, bacon wrapped mushrooms made an appearance, together with delicious apple muffins, hot from the oven. By the time he rose from the table, his lordship's headache was considerably improved, though his temper was still uncertain.

He paced around the room a few times and then came to a decision. He rang the bell and within a couple of minutes Bullock appeared.

"Find young Tom and bring him here," he said curtly.

He did not have long to wait. The butler recognized the signs of his lordship's rare hangover and wasted no time in finding the boy. Tom was ushered in, smelling of the stables, where he had been helping to brush the horses.

"Can you take me to the place you used to work?" asked his employer, without preamble.

Tom blanched. "Why, me lord? You ain't never goin' to send me back? I ain't done nuffin! Monsoor Antoine said as 'ow I could 'ave them bits o' pie. It were left over!" He turned a pitiful face up to him.

In spite of his bad humor, the Earl gave a wan smile. "Nothing like that. I just want to see the place. Go and get the chestnuts poled up and bring 'em round."

"Yessir! Right away!" Tom scampered off and ten minutes later appeared at the front door with the curricle.

Following the boy's somewhat convoluted directions, they arrived at last at the mill. When the Earl directed Tom to stay with the horses, he was relieved. The place he had escaped from still figured in his nightmares and there were nights when he tried not to fall asleep for fear that when he awoke, he would find his new life had been nothing but a dream.

His lordship strode without hesitation into the hot, dust-filled place. The clamor of the machinery smote his sensitive brain and it was with narrowed eyes that he looked around. His arrival was not immediately noticed, but then Mr. Skillins' eye fell upon his tall hat, travelled down his impeccably fitting coat to his tightly fitting trousers and his immaculate boots. He knew Quality when he saw it, and came bustling down from his spot on the platform.

"How may I help you, sir?" he said, bowing as low as his protuberant stomach would allow.

The premises were private property and he knew he had no right to be there. But the Earl was in no mood to be conciliatory. "I am Ailesbury," he said in a tone that brooked no denial, "I wish to see for myself the production in this manufactory."

"Certainly, sir." Mr. Skillins was all geniality, but he remembered the name. "It's an 'onor to see you 'ere, sir. We was visited by a young lady not so long ago. Your secretary, I believe she said she was. She wanted to look around, too. She took away a boy what was… indentured to me. But no matter. We've got nothing to 'ide. A very fine product we makes 'ere. Very fine indeed, as you will see if you step this way."

Under the guise of examining the cotton wound onto the spools, the Earl observed exactly what Amelia had told him. It was impossible to see it had been cleaned a few weeks before. The floors and atmosphere were once more filled with cotton fibers. Sickly young children covered in the white dust crawled beneath the clattering machine; pale, malnourished young women with movements like automatons carried baskets of raw cotton at one end, and loaded full spools at the other. There were windows in the long hall, but they were high up in the walls, too high for effective ventilation. The atmosphere was unbearably hot and damp, the people more like animals than human. Though he had not yet read it, his secretary's comparison of it to a jungle was apt.

"I've seen enough," he said at length. "I'm told it is Lord Smithson who owns this business?"

"Yessir," replied the overseer. "Best cotton in the country and only mill in London."

"I shall be sure to congratulate him when I see him," said the Earl ironically.

When he got home, he went into Amelia's office, found the speech she had written and read it. In spite of his bad temper, he smiled a little at the opening that did, indeed, sound like him, and the conclusion that most certainly did not. He tapped the papers against his thigh for a moment, then decided. Dammit, he would read the speech. Smithson wouldn't like it, but he wasn't mentioned by name and the place was a scene from hell. No gentleman should put people in the position of working like that. Then he remembered his tenants in the flooded cottages. Nor like that, either. He sighed. If he'd known, he never would have engaged that red-headed hornet as his secretary. By God, she stung.

The next morning, Amelia did not come to Albemarle Street. The Earl fought with himself about doing nothing, sending her a note, or driving over to talk to her. He finally convinced himself that writing a letter might be the best option. It would give her time to think before replying. Then he realized he had no idea where she lived. He had engaged her in the street, and his previous secretary had not deemed it necessary to check on her bona fides. Neither he nor anyone else had ever asked where she lived. She always left the house on foot, and Tom, when applied to, said she took a hack at the bottom of the street. He knew no more than that.

Annoyed and frustrated, his lordship at last hit on the idea of looking for her brother at Gentleman Jackson's. He might even be able to find out whether Amelia would be ready to talk to him. She had probably told Aurelius about their disagreement.

It was later than usual when he got to the boxing saloon, and Aurelius was not there. By good fortune, however, a young blade who the Earl had several times seen with the young god was there. He had been introduced to him as Ferdy Brougham. He approached him.

"Forgive my addressing you in this manner," he said to the young man, who was rather ineffectually punching at one of the sawdust-filled leather bags that hug from the ceiling, "but I hope you remember me. I'm Ailesbury. Aurelius Moreton introduced us."

"But, of course," stuttered Ferdy, astonished but gratified at being sought out by one of the senior and most proficient members of the establishment. "Yes... er, sir. How may I be of service to you?"

"Matter of fact it's Moreton I wish to see. Do you know where I might find him?"

The other man bit his lip. "Well, the truth is… er, my lord, he… um… he don't wish to be found just at present."

"Why's that? Been on the cut, has he?"

"Yes, I mean no, no more than usual. He's just, well he ain't fit to be seen."

"He'll be fit enough to be seen by me. Where is he, do you know?"

"Matter of fact, I do. He's at my lodgings, but you don't want to go there."

"Yes, I do. It's imperative that I see him as soon as possible. Can you take me there? My carriage is outside."

The young man shook his head. "I don't know… he won't like…."

The Earl played his trump card. "It's about his sister. He'll want to know."

The ploy succeeded. "Oh, well, in that case…," responded Ferdy. "Just give me a minute to sluice myself down, you know…."

"Certainly. I'll wait here."

It was almost an hour later by the time his lordship's carriage drew up in front of a tall row of houses, obviously cut up into lodgings for single gentlemen. He was let in the front door and led up a staircase that would have been better for a dusting. Ferdy's apartments on the second floor proved to be one long room reaching from the front to the back of the house, the front serving as a living area and the rather gloomy back as sleeping quarters. It was indescribably untidy. Newspapers of the sporting variety and what looked like torn-up betting slips lay all over the floor and the surfaces were covered in a variety of cast-off clothing from fantastically colored waistcoats to top hats, walking canes, whips and single gloves. The dining table was covered with a clutter of dirty plates, mugs and brown bottles.

"The woman hasn't been in yet," explained Ferdy, unnecessarily. Then he called, "Hey, Aury! Lord Ailesbury's here to see you! Something about your sister. Shake a leg, there's a good fellow!"

A mound of blankets moved on one of the couches at the other end of the room and a blond head rose up. It was impossible for Aurelius Moreton to look anything less than god-like, but now he appeared less like Apollo and more like the image etched on a tarnished coin of a young Poseidon rising from the bottom of the sea. He stood up, his garments half on, half off, his curls straggling down his neck, his blue eyes bleary, his face covered in several days' growth of blond beard.

"Ailesbury?" he said. "What about Amelia? Where is she? What have you done to her? Goddam it, if you've...." He lunged and staggered forward or, rather, fell towards the visitor.

The Earl caught him by the wrists and forced him onto a chair. "Nothing, you young fool." he said calmly. "Sit down." Then, turning to his host, "How about some coffee? D'you think that woman of yours can rustle some up?" And to Aurelius, "When did you last eat?" When Aurelius looked blank, he added, "A sandwich, too. Coffee and sandwiches."

Ferdy looked from the one to the other and nodded. "I'll see what I can do," he said and left.

The Earl fixed his eyes on Aurelius. "Why are you here and not at home? Does your sister know where you are? She'll be mad

147

with worry." For one hopeful moment, he wondered if it was her brother's absence rather than their disagreement that had caused her not to come to Albemarle Street that morning.

"Sent her a note. Said I was staying with friends for a few days," he replied sulkily. "So, what did Ferdy mean, you're here because of something to do with Amelia?"

"I… er needed to see you urgently and that was the best excuse I could come up with. But forget that for the moment. What's going on? Why're you looking like something the cat dragged in?"

"What's urgent? Why d'you need to see me?"

The Earl realized there was no reason for this man to confide in him. He was his sister's employer, an acquaintance, nothing more. To his amazement, he heard himself saying, "I… er, I needed to ask you… er, as head of the family, if I could… er, pay her my addresses."

Aurelius stared at him. "Pay her your addresses? You mean…?"

"Marry her. Yes." What in God's name was he doing? What on earth possessed him to tell the younger man that?

His prospective brother-in-law stood up and grabbed him by the hand. "That's the only good news I've had this month!" he said, pumping his arm up and down. Then a realization seemed to hit him. "But you… you won't want a dirty dish like me in the family!" He sat down again and put his head in his hands. "I hope you haven't popped the question yet!" he groaned. "You'll want to back off when you hear about me!"

"What about you? What are you saying, Aurelius? Come on, man out with it!" His lordship sat down next to the younger man, and gripped his broad shoulder.

"I'm… or we, Amy and I, we're completely under the hatches. I lost it all. Everything. Even her portion. She trusted me, you see. Never put any limits on my spending. God knows, she never spends anything on herself."

With an effort, he pulled himself together. "Better begin at the beginning. While she was away with you over Easter, I told her I was engaged with some good chaps and I wasn't going home for the last of the hunting. God! How I wish I'd gone! Thing is, I'd met them over in the sluices. Tothill Fields, you know. Cock fighting. A few wagers, you know how it is. Then a few hands of cards, nothing too serious. I won a few times. Told myself I was a dab hand at the cards, though when I play at home with m'sister, she always beats me. Thought I must be on a run of luck. Then one night I ran into a gentleman – a real one, like yourself. Lord Smithson. He had bet on the same bird as I. At one point it looked as if it was all done in, but then it came back and won like a trooper. We congratulated each other, and he asked if I'd like to have a jar with him. Asked if I'd ever been to Watier's."

The Earl groaned.

"D'you know it, my lord?"

"Yes, and I know the Great Go is not the place for a boy like you. The play has always been pretty deep. Prince Billy himself started it as a supper club with his cook. Years ago it was the haunt of only the highest and richest. You could win or lose a fortune there, but at least the play was honest. But the men who hold the bank nowadays aren't to be trusted. It ought to be shut down."

"Well, Lord Smithson held the bank when I was there. I thought since he was a friend of mine, it'd all be right and tight. And it was. I won at first—Macao, you know. The Devil's game, But then I began to lose. Smithson said I just had to hold firm, come back the next night and I'd come about, But I didn't, I went back and back, hoping to make it up, He ended up with vowels of mine to the tune of ten thousand pounds! Ten thousand pounds! I must have been mad! I was mad! It was like a fever. I don't know how many hours I was there, or whether it was day or night, In the end, when he broke up the last game he said, I trust you will bring what you owe me to my house, I receive visitors in the mornings between ten and eleven. You have three days. It was the voice of a stranger! I thought he was my friend!"

His voice broke. He collected himself then continued, "I thought of giving him the deeds to my estate, but that would leave Amy with no income. So I decided to enlist. She would never hear of me going into the Army you know. Wanted me in the Diplomatic Service. Look at me! The Diplomatic Service!" He laughed hollowly. "But I always wanted to try for a Commission. Can't do that now I'm washed up. But they'd be bound to take me in the ranks, with Boney getting his army together. It'd take a few years, but with what I'd earn and what I could save from the estate, I could come about. So I went to Smithson and tried to persuade him to give me credit. But the way he looked at me! How he spoke to me! He said didn't I know a gentleman always pays his gambling debts immediately. If he'd known I was no gentleman he would never have introduced me to his Club. No gentleman! If my Pa had heard that!" Aurelius broke down completely this time. He sobbed uncontrollably.

With his charm and good looks, Aurelius had never met anyone who wished him ill. Everyone had always been his friend.

He couldn't understand it. The Earl could. The overseer from the mill had obviously told his employer about Amelia's interfering. Someone had no doubt told the peer she had a twin brother. A man who looked like Aurelius Moreton would be easy to find. To get back at the sister, he'd ruined the brother.

But the Earl said none of this. Instead he gripped the young man's shoulder and held it there till he stopped sobbing. Then he said, "Look, Aurelius, there's no sugar-coating this. I've no doubt Smithson is already busy spreading rumors around town about you running away from your gambling debts. He's a bad lot. It'll be all the talk in the clubs. But I can help you come about if you will allow me to pay your debt. As I'm… er, I'm to be a member of the family, there's no shame in that. But any more gossip is bound to get to Amelia's ears, so it's best you leave London immediately. The Army is a good idea. You're right about Wellington needing good men. You wanted a Commission in the Hussars I believe? I can help there. Have you heard of Henry Paget, Lord Uxbridge? He's Commander of the 7th Dragoons, hero of the Peninsular War. He's my Godfather."

He took out his pocket book and, in his habitual scrawl, wrote a few lines on one of his cards. "Here, take this to him. He lives on Ashburton Place. I've told him I'll purchase a Commission for you into the 7th. And take this, for immediate expenses." He handed the younger man the card and a roll of banknotes.

Then he continued. "But Amelia must know nothing of this. Write her a letter today saying you had the opportunity of a Commission from Lord Uxbridge himself. You met him at a dinner a week ago, and he remembered your father. They were at school together, or some such. Make up some story. He asked you to leave at once, as they are urgently preparing to defend against Bonaparte. It's true the members of the Vienna Congress have bound themselves to each put 150,000 men into the field for the inevitable conflict."

"Good Lord! Don't I know it!" cried Aurelius, a light blazing in his eyes. "The fellow returned to Paris just last month. He's already established a new Charter for the people. They all adore him!"

"Well, perhaps not quite all," responded the Earl, drily. "But he certainly is a devil when it comes to engaging the populace."

"And his men," said Aurelius, his disgraceful losses momentarily forgotten and his old enthusiasm returning. "They say Louis left with only 46,000 men ready to campaign, and he has already increased it up to over 100,000."

"So Uxbridge will be glad to have you," said his lordship, rising from his seat. "But for God's sake, clean yourself up before you go to see him!"

Aurelius laughed and pumped his hand, "I shall never be able to repay you, sir. You're the best brother-in-law a man could ask for."

"As to that, keep it mum for the moment. Don't go blabbing it to anyone, I haven't asked Amelia yet. There's no guarantee she'll say yes."

"Good Lord! If she don't say yes, I'll eat my... my new busby! If you ask me, she's been in love with you from the start. I know because she don't talk about you much and when anyone mentions your name, she colors up. Never known her to do that!"

His lordship had no leisure to consider the implication of that remark because at that moment, Ferdy returned with his landlady. He was carrying a tray with coffee and three cups. She had a pile of ham sandwiches each about three inches thick.

"Sorry for the delay. Mrs. P had to go and get some ham. Not a bit of meat in the house."

"Sorry I can't stay to enjoy it," said his lordship, who wanted to go home and think. "Got an appointment." Then he clapped his hand to his forehead. "Nearly forgot, I need your direction, Aurelius. I seem to have... er, lost it. Write it down for me, there's a good chap, Papers, you know...," he added vaguely.

So while his imagined brother-in-law wrote down the twins' London address, the Earl watched the landlady make an ineffective push to clean up the dining table by simply piling all the plates into a wobbling heap at one end. He was glad he wouldn't be there for the inevitable crash. He made his way back to Albemarle Street wondering all the way how he was going to persuade Miss Moreton to marry him when he had just paid for her brother to take up the very profession she was determined he should not have.

Chapter Twenty

The following afternoon, Amelia received two letters. The first was from her employer. He was almost certainly releasing her from her employment. Nevertheless, she was unable to suppress a fond smile at his appalling handwriting. The sooner he got a new secretary, the better, she thought. However, she was to be surprised.

23 Albemarle Street, London
Tuesday the 11th of April
Dear Miss Moreton,

After your departure yesterday I visited Tom's erstwhile place of employment. The effect it had on me was exactly the same as upon you. You were right to bring my attention to the working conditions in these places, as you were right to show me the problem with the river cottages at Deering.

I must be either a very fearsome fellow or a very indolent one for you to have decided not to tell me you had signed me up for my Maiden Speech until you thought it was too late for me to cry off. You see, I know you well enough to be aware that is what you did. Since no one has ever accused me of being fearsome, I am left with the sad conclusion you think me indolent. This accords, too, with how my mother says you described me.

But it is precisely because I am such a useless individual that I must I beg you to return to Albemarle Street. Writing this letter myself has exhausted me to the point I need to repair to bed for a week. Besides, Tom misses you.

But of course, I cannot allow myself any repose until after I deliver my Maiden Speech tomorrow. How my knees do knock at the prospect! If only there were some way you could do it for me, as you have done everything else, with efficiency and good humor. Please return to wish me good luck. I may never be the same again.

Yours, etc.,
Ailesbury

Amelia laughed as she read this letter and a huge weight was lifted off her heart. She had thought on Monday that she might never see the Earl again. She had cried herself to sleep that night, a thing she had not done since the death of her parents.

The second letter was from her brother. It completely wiped the smile from her face, After reading the first two lines, she threw it to the floor and leaped up, crying "No! No! Oh Aury, what have you done?" and burst into tears. It was lucky her aunt was out, for it took her several minutes of angry pacing, the tears pouring from her eyes, before she could gain enough control of herself to pick up the letter and read the rest.

En Route to Belgium, the 11th of April 1815

Dear Amy,

You will be astonished when you read my direction, but it is true! I'm on my way to join a

156

garrison of the Hussars to be dispatched against Boney. I can't give you more details. Secret, you know. You won't believe my luck! At dinner last week I ate my mutton next to Lord Uxbridge. Do you know him? I don't, or at least I didn't. He's Commander of the 7th Dragoons. When I introduced myself he got all excited. It seems he was at school with Pa and always owed him a favor. Didn't tell me what, of course, and I didn't ask. Not the thing, you know. Asked me how Pa was doing and when I told him, he was fair blue-devilled, I can tell you. Anyway, the upshot was he asked if there was anything he could do for me instead. I told him I was mighty keen on a Commission in the Hussars, and he said he'd arrange it for me. I told you I was staying with Ferdy, didn't I? Stout fellow! By God, the next day at his place I got a message to go to his office and they shipped me off right away! Didn't even have time to come home to say goodbye. With Boney preparing for war, everything is moving mighty fast I can tell you!

So here I am, my dear. I don't know when I'll be home but don't worry. I'll do what you said, ask myself would Amy do this, and if the answer is no, I won't.

Send my love to Aunt Edna. Wait till you both see me in my uniform!

Your most affectionate brother,
Aurelius Moreton

P.S. Hang onto that Earl of yours. He's a Trojan.

When she had fully grasped the contents of the whole letter, she sank into a chair and covered her eyes with her hands. What on earth had persuaded Aury to do anything so outrageous? He knew she didn't want him to go into the Army! He knew! But then, as her breathing slowed and she could think more clearly, she understood that was the real reason he hadn't come home. She would have done her best to persuade him against taking the Commission, and being the amenable soul he was, he would probably have agreed.

As she sat there, trying to make sense of it all, she was finally forced to admit that she was an abominable, managing kind of woman. She was! She made people do what they didn't want, because she felt she knew better. She had always bullied—yes bullied Aurelius, just as he had said! He hadn't wanted to go to Oxford. He hadn't wanted to go into the Diplomatic Service. She had simply overridden his feelings and substituted them with her own! And she had done the same to the Earl! She knew he wouldn't want to make a speech in the House, But she had thought it important. He was only doing what she had forced him into because of his breeding. It would not allow him to go back on his word, even when the word wasn't really his. And the same breeding was cloaking it in good humored banter. After a lifetime of feeling she was always in the right of things, this was a very sobering reflection.

Calmer now, she read the letter through again. Though her heart still sank at the thought of her beloved brother on the battlefield, she told herself that surely Lord Uxbridge, who owed something to their father (odd that he had never mentioned it!) would keep an eye on his son. And what did he mean by that reference to the Earl? What had he to do with the matter? She puzzled over it for a moment and then gave up. He was probably referring to the boxing saloon.

By the time her aunt returned, Amelia was able to share the contents of Aury's letter in a calm voice, and even encourage her to think it a good thing.

"For you know, Aunt," she said. "He was beginning to worry me. Out till all hours and looking queer as Dick's hatband these last few weeks. The Army will be good for him. Regular hours, lots of exercise. You wait, when he comes back he'll have side whiskers and be quite stout!"

Both women tried to laugh at this picture of their beloved Aurelius. Then, for fear of breaking into tears, they both spent the rest of the afternoon and evening attempting to concentrate on something else and resolutely leaving unuttered all the dreadful thoughts that flooded them.

The following morning, Amelia made her way a little late to Albemarle Street, where she was greeted joyously by Tom, who had been watching for her. She had hoped and not hoped his lordship might already have left, but he came out of his office and greeted her with a smile. He noticed her drawn expression but did not comment upon it, sure it was due to her brother's departure. Instead, he said he'd waited to ask if she would accompany him to the House and sit in the Visitor's Gallery during his speech. He said laughingly she could berate him afterwards if he made a poor showing of it.

"Oh, my lord," she said, in a tone very different from usual, "I don't think I can blame anyone ever again for making a poor showing of anything. I've recently come to the realization I've been mistaken in a number of things." And she turned away before he could see her eyes fill with tears.

"I find that impossible to believe," he said, still in the same jocular manner, though he was very aware of the tremble in her voice.

"My brother has joined the Army with a Commission in Lord Uxbridge's Regiment and is even now on his way to Belgium," she said, all in a rush, fearful of breaking down, her back still towards him. "And he didn't tell me he was leaving."

"Then he is to be congratulated!" replied the Earl in a kindly tone, "You told me once that was his desire. He'll see some action and come home victorious."

"If he comes home," said Amelia with a sob, "I wish I had known how set he was upon it."

"Why? Would you have tried to talk him out of it?"

"Yes," she said in a small voice, "I would. That's one of the things I've been mistaken about, I had decided he should be a diplomat and imagined he agreed with me." She turned to him, her chin up. "The other is obliging you to make a Maiden Speech. I knew you wouldn't like it, but I went on regardless."

"But Miss Moreton," he replied gently, "as I told you in my letter, I went to the factory and saw for myself what you meant. I think it's right to make that speech. If I hadn't wanted to, I assure you I would simply have sent a note to the House to say I was indisposed. You did not make me do anything. I may be indolent and frivolous, but I do have a mind of my own."

"It is very kind of you to explain it like that, but…," she began.

"But you don't believe me?" He laughed. "When you know me better, you will see I'm every bit as stubborn as you, though perhaps less direct about it. Now," he took her hand, "will you come with me? I should hate to be late."

Amelia had not taken off her bonnet and pelisse, so allowed herself to be led outside and handed into the curricle.

"I think I will have you drive, Miss Moreton," he said. "It suits my sense of dignity on such an occasion. But pray, do not gallop, It would not be dignified at all if I were to fall off."

Amelia knew he was trying to cheer her up and gave him a rather watery smile. She clicked up the horses and drove at a very sedate pace to the Houses of Parliament,

So it was that Lord Smithson, arriving at the House in his carriage, was treated to the sight of Miss Moreton ably threading the Earl of Ailesbury's carriage though the traffic on the parterre in front of the Houses of Parliament. The main buildings were an odd combination of medieval turreted castle and Italian arcade, together with the neo-gothic Lords building tacked gratuitously on the side. It had been the primary residence of the Kings of England until much of it was burned in the early sixteenth century. It had been rebuilt piecemeal, which accounted for its curious appearance. The Earl and his driver were, however, oblivious to this and merely handed the reins to Tom.

For his part, Lord Smithson was much more interested in Miss Moreton than in the history of the building into which he now made his way. He had no trouble recognizing her from Skillins' description. Her fiery red hair was escaping, as always, from its pins. His triumph in embroiling her brother in gambling debts had proved short lived. He had been surprised and not gratified the day before to receive a package containing ten thousand pounds in bank notes from the young fool. A note with it had simply said, *My compliments and apologies for the delay*, with a scrawled signature. He wondered where he had found the money. He'd been looking forward to seeing him snubbed by the ton and refused entry into any of the Clubs, but he had not put in an appearance. Besides, it seemed he had many friends. Lord Smithson had found himself criticized more often than not for having allowed the young man to get into so much trouble. No one was ignorant of the deep play and suspicious activities at Watier's. His eyes narrowed when he saw Miss Moreton go towards the Visitors' Gallery. He wondered if she knew what trouble her brother had been in.

The Earl of Ailesbury was the first order of business that Thursday morning. The Speaker opened the session and invited him to address the house. His lordship did so, standing straight but relaxed. He began with a gleam of humor in his eye and pronounced the words exactly as Amelia had written them. He paused for the laughter, and glanced up at her in the Visitors' Gallery. Sitting up there, she was acutely aware both of the strength of his personality, and the handsome figure he presented. When he looked up at her, her heart leaped.

Once the serious part of the speech began, his tone became more solemn. He spoke in an even, carrying voice, hardly glancing at the paper in his hand, looking round at his fellow peers. There were nods of agreement as he outlined the shortcomings of the earlier Factory Act and murmuring and shuffling of feet as he described the scene in the factory on the Thames. When he came to the conclusion, he again used Amelia's words exactly as she had written them, ascribing to the factory the horrors of the jungle and accusing a member of the chamber of being complicit in them. At this, the members of the House looked around at each other and muttered. When his last words rang out, urging the creation of an Act that would allow working children to grow up in health and security and make them bless forever the names of the men who proposed it, there was a moment of complete silence. Then the House rose in applause almost as one. Lord Smithson was the only member reluctant to stand and as soon as was possible in the congratulatory throng, he jammed his hat upon his head and walked swiftly from the Chamber. This did not pass unnoticed. It was not long before word was running around the chamber as to who was the owner of the mill on the Thames.

The Earl could hardly remove himself before the other affairs of the day were completed, so Amelia remained in the Visitors' Gallery. At first she watched with great interest. Apparently, the Prime Minister (the Earl of Liverpool) had received an overture of peace from Bonaparte and the Duke of Norfolk inquired as to whether the House might know the terms. As he referred to the Frenchman as *Buonaparte*, it was a minute before Amelia knew who he was talking about. In any case, the answer from the Prime Minister was No. The overture had been transmitted to the Congress in Vienna and no report could be made until word had been received from them. The British Government would have no direct communication with the present ruler of France. Amelia thought immediately about her brother, en route for Belgium and destined for confrontation with the French forces, and hoped against hope that Bonaparte's overtures might be accepted. Then Aurelius could come home, none the worse for wear.

Her interest waned during a very long speech that followed. The Marquis of Wellesley, who obviously liked the sound of his own voice, delivered a lengthy oration in support of a motion regarding the negotiation for peace with America. What exactly the motion was, she was never to know. She understood that the Emperor of Russia had been proposed as a mediator between the parties, but this had been rejected. Then he went on to make rather obscure comments about whether the natural boundaries between countries could be compared to those between

America, which was now independent, and Canada, which continued to be a British territory. He charged America with unbounded ambition, as manifested by her acquisition of Louisiana not more than eleven years before. After that, Amelia began to lose the thread of the argument. The last few nights her repose had been broken by worries about her brother and the Earl; the Gallery was stuffy and she fell asleep. She awoke only when the vote was called. The motion, whatever it had been, was defeated by 83 to 30, She noticed that the Earl voted no. She would ask him later what it had all been about.

It was almost four in the afternoon when the House finally rose. Amelia had eaten no lunch and nearly no breakfast, so she was by now very hungry. When she saw the Earl leave his place, she went downstairs to meet him. He was evidently held back by a stream of well-wishers, for it was some minutes before he found her, pressed against the wall.

"I hope you're satisfied that I have done my civic duty, Miss Moreton," he said. "Now you see why I come here as rarely as possible, Wellesley's speech was exactly what I seek to avoid, and don't you dare to remonstrate with me! You were asleep for most of it! Don't pretend you weren't!"

"It was very warm up there," was all the excuse his secretary could offer, "And I couldn't follow it. But I was awake for your speech. It was very fine."

His lordship laughed, "But you wrote it!"

"I know, but it was much better when you said it. It didn't sound like my words at all!" Then she said, "What was Lord Wellesley's motion?"

"I have no idea. But Stanhope supported it and he's a fool. Whatever he supports I do the opposite."

"So that is democracy in action!" laughed Amelia, "I'm asleep and you vote against whatever another votes for!"

"Exactly. Come on, let's go and have a cup of tea. Or something stronger. We've earned it!"

Chapter Twenty-One

Life at number 23 Albemarle Street now continued much as it had before except that Amelia worried continually about her brother. She had heard nothing more from him since that letter and scoured the newspapers daily. Remembering the speech about the French General she had heard in the House, she kept looking for reports some sort of peace had been agreed in Vienna. But there was nothing. The fact was, the parlays between Bonaparte and Vienna had failed.

His lordship continued his usual round of amusements, accepted or rejected by Amelia on his behalf. Word came from Mr. Bright that building on the new river cottages had begun and he hoped next time Miss Moreton came to Deering she would see the improvements that had been made. The bills for the first quarter arrived and were paid; she was pleased to see the candle and coal consumption was significantly reduced. Life, in short, ran on oiled wheels.

The Earl often came into her office for no particular reason. He sat back in the chair opposite her, pushing away from the desk with his long legs. He said he liked to watch her work. It made him feel useful, giving her so much to do. She still kept her pen stuck in her hair and would pull it out for him to sign things, since he was there. He complained that it meant sitting upright, and he was comfortable where he was, and couldn't she sign for him. She often did so, shaking her head at his unbelievable indolence.

They were almost like an old married couple, the way they laughed at the same things and could also sit saying nothing, perfectly comfortable in each other's company. The Earl's feelings for her grew into love, but he was reticent to declare himself. Though he genuinely believed it was for the best, the knowledge it was he who had paid for her brother's Commission weighed on his conscience. He would have to confess it, and then she would probably never want to talk to him again. Rather than risk that, he said nothing.

One evening the Earl was playing cards with a group of friends at his Club when a new member asked to join their table. His name, he said, was Hugo Munson. He was a friend of... and he recited a number of names known to them. One was Smithson. He had recently returned from India, where he had been involved in the tea plantations. His wife had passed away and he had decided to retire back to England. He played reasonably well, was of an amiable disposition and seemed as happy losing as winning. He soon became a fixture at their table.

As it will when men get together, the talk often turned to horses. Munson said that in India he was held to be a reasonable whip, though he didn't know how he would fare on the English roads. He had had a racing curricle built, he said, and was eager to try it out. His challenge was taken up by some of the others, and news came of a few friendly races on Hampstead Heath or Moorfields. Munson indeed proved himself no mean whip and won rather more often than he lost, though more than once he commented he needed better horses. He'd bought his pair when he first arrived in England, but now thought he'd been choused. Then he arrived at the Club one evening with the news he had purchased the sweetest pair of greys.

"I was damned lucky," he said. "Happened to be at Tattersall's when Sansome came in, He was selling his pair." This was a name known to the group, Verwood Sansome was the young heir to a fortune he was doing his best to spend as fast as he could, even before he came into it. His father, knowing his son's proclivities, had had the foresight before his death to put the family money into the hands of a very conservative man of business until his son should reach the age of twenty-five. By that time, it was hoped, he would have learned how to live within his means. The *on-dit* was that young Sansome had suffered heavy losses at play and the man of business so sensibly chosen by his father was absolutely refusing to extend him any more before the end of the quarter. Since they were only in April, he had over two months to go. His debts had to be paid. The Earl vividly remembered Aurelius's dilemma in the same situation. Sansome had to sell his greys.

The assembled group exclaimed on Munson's good fortune. They were less sympathetic with Sansome, who was known to be a young fool. They all knew the greys. A fine pair.

"Yes," said Munson, "Now I'm of a mind to try them out. I'm told the London to Brighton Road is a good test. Anyone care to take me on?"

There was silence. They all knew he'd done well enough with his old pair, and with Sansome's greys, he might be well nigh unbeatable. Then a voice from the other side of the room called out. It was Lord Smithson.

"What about you, Ailesbury? You have a neatish pair of chestnuts. Don't you care to set them against Sansome's greys? Or is it that you don't like the competition with Munson himself? And I thought you were considered a Nonpareil!"

He came towards the table with a smile on his face that didn't reach his eyes, He had been a rare visitor to the Club these last weeks. He had never been able to score off the red-headed secretary after her brother paid his debts and disappeared. After the Earl had exposed him in the House, his attitude towards the whole Ailesbury establishment had hardened into positive dislike. He had had an uncomfortable time since the Maiden Speech. The Earl was such a well-known character that it had been reported in The Times. When the newspaper had contacted his lordship about it, Amelia, who was of course the one who handled the request, had sent them a copy of the whole discourse. It had been printed in its entirety and everyone had read it.

The weavers in Spitalfields had read it too, and had been making a noise about removing their custom. They were threatening to get their cotton from the North. The conditions in the mills were probably no better, but they had heard from the merceries they supplied that more than one of the socialites who bought their cotton had asked if it came from "that dreadful place Lord Ailesbury spoke about". In the end, Smithson had only kept their business by much reducing the price.

Then a chance encounter with Hugo Munson gave him an idea. Just arrived home from India, Munson commented that he enjoyed a flutter on a horse race between friends. Apparently this had been a common entertainment in India in the dry season. Smithson befriended and encouraged him, putting him up for a membership at White's, where the Earl was known to play cards with his friends. He told him the men there were generally keen on a friendly wager. It was he who had suggested the fifty-two-mile London to Brighton road. The Prince Regent had made it popular for races. It was well-maintained and there were a number of posting houses where the ostlers could be relied on to change the horses with lightning speed.

"You're mighty quiet, Ailesbury!" he said now. "I never heard you refuse a challenge before! Crying craven?"

The Earl looked up at him. The man had never been one of his intimates, and since the affair with young Moreton, his mistrust had deepened into positive dislike. However, he replied with his usual calm, "Not at all, I was just waiting to see if anyone else wanted to step in. If not, I'm happy to have a friendly wager with you, Munson, What do you say to five hundred pounds on it? Clapham Common to Georgy's place."

"Better make it the Chapel Royal, old man," said one of the men around the table. "Nash is making a hell of a mess of the Regent's palace with his architectural flights of fancy. It's looking like a cross between an exhibition hall and a seraglio. Don't go near it."

"Done! Clapham Common to The Chapel Royal!" cried Munson. "Five hundred it is. When?"

"A week today," replied the Earl. "Next Wednesday, the...," he calculated, "the 14th of May. If we leave at nine in the morning, we should be in Brighton for lunch. Someone bring over the book."

The wager was duly entered into the book, underneath the numerous and often ludicrous bets that members had placed there for years. These included bets as to which raindrop would reach the bottom of the windowpane first, the date on which Lady This or Countess That would be delivered of a child, and whether it would be a boy or a girl, and how many cherries Lord X could consume before the Earl of Y finished his glass of port. Nevertheless, however ridiculous, once a bet had been registered it was sacrosanct. As a matter of honor, no gentleman could cry off.

The wager soon became widely known amongst the ton, not least because everywhere he went, Lord Smithson promoted it. The two parties were held to be fairly evenly matched, which made for spirited discussions. Munson was a newcomer but his success in previous races and the known quality of Sansome's greys made him a worthy adversary for the Earl. For his part, though generally held to be one of the finest whips in the country, his lordship hadn't raced his chestnuts recently and there might be a possibility they were a little stale. As the week went on the odds veered first one way then the other, and the amount of money staked grew to astronomical proportions.

Amelia first learned about the wager from Tom, who, in turn, had it from the other grooms and tigers he hobnobbed with while waiting with his lordship's horses. They were always amongst the first to know everything. Betting was as ferocious between them as between the gentlemen in the clubs, though the sums involved were, necessarily, smaller.

"I laid a sovereign on 'is lordship meself," said Tom. "They's getting 'is racing curricle out o' the mews and it's a beauty. Wiv 'im driving that and the chestnuts, there ain't no one can beat 'im. You gonna lay a bet, Miss Moreton?"

"Certainly not, though I agree with you, Tom. Even without seeing the other gentleman's equipage, or, indeed his lordship's racing vehicle, I'm sure you're right."

She mentioned it to the Earl a few hours later. He replied, in his usual careless manner, "Oh that? Yes, damned stupid thing. But since we're on the topic, if we leave here at nine, we should be in Brighton not long after one. Write to the White Horse Inn and bespeak a private room and luncheon for me, would you? I may as well enjoy a decent meal at the end of it. Not that it will be a patch on Antoine's," he ended gloomily.

She later heard he had asked Tom to go along with him to blow the yard of tin. When she next saw the boy, he was almost speechless with joy at the prospect. She told him he'd be able to see the sea and he turned eyes of wonder upon her.

"The sea? You mean with fishes and all?"

"Yes," she laughed. "But please don't go in to look for the fish. I'm afraid you might drown. The waves can catch you unawares!" She guessed, quite rightly, that a London bred boy would never have learned to swim.

Chapter Twenty-Two

The ease that now existed between Miss Moreton and her employer was to receive a devastating check. On the Monday before the now-famous race, she was, as usual, opening his lordship's post, when she saw one from the Office of the Commander of the 7th Dragoons. Any mention of the Dragoons immediately brought Aurelius to mind, and she opened it in some trepidation. Her bewildered gaze fell on the following:

His Majesty's 7th Dragoons
Regimental Headquarters
York
The 1st of May 1815

To:

Purchase of Lieutenant's Commission for Aurelius Moreton ... £2,050

To be Held as Bond against Good Behavior and made available to the Bond Holder on the Occasion of his Retirement or Honorable Discharge.

By Order of His Lordship,
First Marquess of Anglesey, Earl of Uxbridge

She sat looking at this for some minutes, her mind in turmoil of unanswered questions. Why had this bill for Aurelius's Commission been sent to the Earl? What had he to do with it? Then she recalled her brother's postscript: hang onto to that Earl of yours. He's a Trojan. She hadn't understood what it meant. All at once, she remembered the Earl's questioning as to whether Aury really wanted to go into the diplomatic service and his easy acceptance of her brother's departure. It was obvious! It was he who had offered to pay for her brother's Commission! Aurelius's story about a friend of their father's had been pure invention! But why? Why had her brother done such a thing, and why had Ailesbury aided him? A sudden burst of rage flooded her.

She seized the letter and stormed out of her office. She knew her employer was taking a late breakfast. Without knocking, she threw open the dining room door and cast the letter onto his lordship's plate.

"Kindly explain what this means!" she said heatedly. "Why are you receiving a bill for Aurelius's Commission?"

"Miss Moreton," came her employer's calm reply, "please won't you...."

"No I won't! And don't calmly Miss Moreton me! I want an answer!" She was shouting now.

"Miss Moreton, Amelia, I'd like to explain if you would just...."

"No! I won't just anything. Tell me! Did you purchase a Commission for my brother?"

The Earl had stood when she came in and now took her elbow. She furiously shook him off.

"Don't you dare touch me! Just tell me. Did you?"

He gave up. "Yes, I did. But...."

"But what? But what?" Amelia's rage was now completely uncontrolled. "You thought he would be better off facing Napoleon's cannons than doing what I wanted? You thought, after a few sessions of silly boxing that you knew him better than

I? You thought because you're a man (and this she spat out with indescribable scorn) you knew better than I, a poor woman?"

She turned on her heel and marched to the open door. Bullock and two footmen were standing there, their mouths agape. She looked at them, then back at the Earl.

"Well," she said in a voice trembling with emotion, "I wish you good luck. I wish you good luck with a staff that sells the household candles to pay for Christmas bonuses, that burns coal in empty rooms in August, that allows the chef to throw away perfectly good food because there was an error in its preparation you probably wouldn't even notice, and gives him free access to drink himself silly with wine from your cellars. I wish you good luck with your useless life, where the most important decision is who you sit next to at dinner, where you make love to stupid women who misspell eight words out of ten in a simple note, where you buy jewelry because you're too weak to say no, and where the latest glorious endeavor is engaging in an idiotic horse race to a town you have no wish to visit. Well, I hope you lose! I hope you fall off your racing curricle and break your neck! I hope you go for a swim and drown!"

Her lip trembling with a fury she could no longer find words to express, her flaming curls tumbling into her face, she ran through the hall, wrenched open the front door and threw herself into the street.

Edward Woodbridge, Earl of Ailesbury, third Baron of Mayne sat down in his chair with a thud. Never in his life had he beheld a woman so magnificently angry, her bosom heaving with such gloriously uncontrolled emotion. Never in his life had he been subjected to such a tirade of abuse. He couldn't help it. He knew he should not, but it was stronger than he. It roiled up from the

177

depth of his being. He put his head back and laughed and laughed till he cried.

When his lordship at last controlled himself, Bullock came in and said hesitatingly, "My lord, I hope Miss Moreton's words have not given you reason to doubt the appropriateness of... arrangements in the house. She spoke about...."

"Yes, yes, Bullock," said his lordship, beginning to laugh again, "she spoke about candles and c...coal and w...wine from my cellars... I kn...know." He stopped and collected himself. "Not to mention I apparently make love to women who can't spell, and buy jewelry to keep them quiet, and make s...silly w...wagers on r...races to B...Brighton." He had to stop again. "But not to worry. We can muddle along with our coal, our candles and our depleted wine cellars. I may have to re-think my choice of female companionship, however. My God! What a magnificent woman!"

"Er... yes, my lord, as you say," mumbled the butler, bowing out of the room not knowing whether to be relieved because his shortcoming had been overlooked, or worried because his employer seemed to have lost his mind.

Amelia, meanwhile, marched furiously almost a mile, hatless and coatless, her hair in a tumble like a madwoman, people turning to look at her in amazement, before hailing a hack and being driven home. She had to keep the driver waiting as she ran indoors to beg money from her aunt, as she had left her reticule, along with everything else, in her office.

Needless to say, her aunt was astonished at her wild appearance, her lack of coat, bonnet and reticule. Amelia invented a story about having been set upon by footpads after leaving her employer. Then she had to calm down her cries of horror and tearful declaration that Amelia must never again set foot in such a lawless location. Her niece was only too ready to agree.

"Don't worry, Aunt. I'm never going back. There's no need, anyway. I was only working for Aury's sake, and that's all over now."

Then she burst into tears. This was so unlike her that her aunt sent her immediately to bed with a tisane and a small dose of laudanum, saying she was suffering from severe shock, and no wonder. Not generally amenable to being physicked, Amelia was feeling so overturned that she took the dose, and consequently slept several hours.

When she awoke in the dark early hours, the full extent of her misery came to her. Her brother was gone and likely to be killed. He had left without saying goodbye because she was so hard to deal with. She had raged at the man she at last admitted she loved. He would never speak to her again. He was probably congratulating himself at having rid himself of a harridan. She knew how she was when she lost her temper. When she remembered what she'd said to him, she shuddered in embarrassment. She lay miserably in bed, watching the dawn gradually lighten the sky, wishing she could stay there forever.

She wasn't surprised when her employer didn't send her things the next day. In fact, she was glad. She didn't feel capable of inventing a reason for the return of what she'd told her aunt had been stolen. The Earl was probably so angry at her outburst that he'd told the housekeeper to put her things on the fire. That's what she would have done. But here she wronged him. He left her belongings where they were, thinking they might force her to return. He had no intention of sending her things to her.

He did, however, send her a letter. It was a model of what his nanny would have called telling the truth with an almost-lie.

23 Albemarle Street, London
The 13th of May, 1815
Dear Miss Moreton,

Your precipitate departure from my home yesterday did not allow me to offer you any explanation for my actions regarding your brother. Please allow me to do that now.

After our last contretemps (my goodness, we do seem to misunderstand each other quite regularly!) I realized I did not have your direction and set out to find your brother to obtain it.

I found him at last hiding in his friend's lodgings in despair over some gambling debts he had unwisely incurred. He had decided to enlist in Wellington's Army, that being the only way he could see to repay his debts. He was not to be dissuaded. I was, however, able to persuade him to accept a Commission I would be able to obtain for him through my godfather, Lord Uxbridge. I thought you would find that infinitely preferable to his engaging as an enlisted man.

I gather he had to leave immediately and sent you a letter to explain. We had agreed he would not mention my part in the affair, for fear of your feeling some sort of indebtedness to me. That would have been embarrassing to us both. Your many justified criticisms of me yesterday have shown that

indebtedness is not, however, your prevailing
sentiment.

I'm sure you have by now realized you left your
possessions here. They are awaiting your return,
which I hope will not be long delayed.

Yours etc.
Ailesbury

Tears came again to Amelia's eyes as she read this letter. She understood now why Aurelius had been looking so haggard before he went away. The poor boy must have been dreadfully worried, so worried he didn't want her to see him. That's why he had gone to stay with his friend instead of coming home. And his lordship was right. If her brother had to join the Army, it was far better he do so with a Commission. She should feel indebted to him, but instead she had said all those awful things. She was so miserable for the rest of the day that her aunt began to be seriously worried and spoke about calling in Dr. Murray.

The next day was the day of the Earl's race to Brighton. Knowing he would be gone early, Amelia steeled herself to go to Albemarle Street and pick up her things. She would write a brief note of thanks to him, and leave a word of goodbye to Tom, then that would be that. She need never see any of them again.

Chapter Twenty-Three

The Earl had arisen at six that morning and dressed in his riding coat, britches and topboots. Before breakfast, he walked hatless around to the mews to examine his racing curricle one last time and look over the chestnuts. He did not notice a pair of gentlemen in mufflers lounging next to an unremarkable carriage, though if he had, and thought about it, he would have wondered why anyone would need a muffler on what promised to be a fine May morning. Having satisfied himself that everything was just as it should be, he was strolling back, thinking about a plate of eggs and ham, when he was set upon from behind. He was a big man and handy with his fists, but he had no time to use them before he felt a heavy blow on the back of his head. His legs crumpled under him. He was caught by a pair of strong arms on either side and hustled within seconds inside the unremarkable carriage.

When he came to, he found himself lying on a pile of sacks in a dark, damp room that, as his head cleared, he realized was probably a cellar. A little light came through a small window set high in the wall. But very little daylight was able to penetrate its filthy panes. He sat up and his head swam. The vile odor of the place struck his nose and he had to sit perfectly still with his eyes shut to overcome the bile that rose to his gorge, making him want to vomit. After a few minutes the sensation passed and he was able to open his eyes. The smell was that of damp overlaid with the rot of decaying fish and vegetation. He must be down by the river. This was confirmed as his eyes became accustomed to the gloom and he saw lengths of rope and twine lying between old packing cases with moldy illustrated labels advertising their one-time contents. He recognized crates for tea, cocoa, rice and sugar. He must be in the cellar of a store house where ships had been offloaded. Since nothing was remotely recent, he guessed the storehouse was no longer in operation.

Why had he been captured and by whom? But the minute he started thinking about it, it was obvious. Smithson! Of course! He wanted him to be dishonored by not showing up for the race to Brighton. It was Smithson who'd urged him into the race to start with. Was Munson involved? He didn't think so. The man might be a bit of an idiot with his mind full of nothing but wagers and races, but he wasn't a poltroon.

Gingerly, he stood up and heard scurrying in the corners. Rats. That was all he needed. He swayed on his feet and his head throbbed at first, but he was soon able to walk slowly around the confines of his cell. There was a stout oak door set in one wall. He pressed his ear to it, but heard nothing. He was going to shout for help but then thought better of it. He retained the shadowy memory of being held on both sides, so he must have had two captors. If they were outside they might open the door, but in his weakened state he would not be able to deal with them. And if he tried once and failed, they might bind him up, making any further attempt impossible. Better to let them think he was still out cold.

They weren't about to do him any real harm, he was persuaded, or they would have done it already. No, they would probably just keep him there until it was obvious he'd missed the race, and then let him go. He'd be forced to slink back home and ultimately meet the accusing and scornful gaze of the ton. Well, by God, he'd get out and run the damned race, even if he came in miles behind.

His captors would probably look in on him at some point to make sure he wasn't dead. It would be human nature to be worried. They'd hit him hard. He felt the bump on the back of his head and winced. He walked around one more time, thinking. Then he got hold of a few lengths of thinnish rope that had probably been around the packing cases, and tied them together till it was long enough to reach from side to side of the room. As quietly as he could, he moved aside wooden crates, packing cases and débris, causing shadowy creatures to scatter – he'd been right about the rats – until he found the strong wooden ceiling supports on either side of the room. He attached the rope securely to one side about eight inches from the floor, and stretched it taut across to the other. It was so dark in the room the rope was invisible unless you were looking for it. Then he sat down to wait.

It seemed interminable. Looking at his timepiece which, miraculously, had been left on his person, he cursed as the hands wound around to eight then nine, then half past. Finally, he heard a bolt sliding on the other side of the door, and lay down on the malodorous sacks facing the door. He groaned artistically but did not move as the door opened and his captors came in.

"Gawd!" he heard one of them say. "'E ain't 'ardly come to. I told yer not to 'it 'im too 'ard, Albert! Me lord Smithson said not to kill 'im, just lay 'im out."

"I din't, Bernie! I din't! I just give 'im a tap wiv me billy!" whined his accomplice.

"Yeah! But these Nobs is soft. Their 'eads ain't used to it. They lays on fevver pillers all their lives."

His lordship made a mental note of his captors' names and his hands involuntarily made fists when he heard them say Smithson. "I'll show them soft," thought the Earl, opening his eyes in narrow slits. The men started into the room, one close behind the other. When his shins encountered the trip rope, the first let out a bellow and fell forward, quickly followed by the other who was too close behind to stop himself. The Earl sprang up before the first man had hit the floor and in a quick stride was next to them both. The second had come in with his club, presumably thinking he might need it again. It fell to the ground with a clatter. His lordship picked it up, and before the men had any idea what was happening, he smacked them both sharply on the back of the head. They collapsed in an inert heap.

"Sleep tight, my hearties," he said under his breath, as he cautiously left the cellar, carrying the club with him. There might be more of them, he thought.

But in the event, having quickly found the stone stairs leading to ground level, he met no one. His eyes were at first dazzled by the bright May morning as he came up into a courtyard. But he was soon able to recognize the place as the yard in front of the cotton mill. He had been right that the storehouse was no longer in use. Smithson must have bought the premises and converted them.

Conscious of being hatless and still carrying the cudgel, the Earl walked swiftly to the cobbled street beyond the gates to the yard and started walking west. He didn't hold out much hope of finding a hackney in the East End, unless one had been hired to bring a passenger down here and it was on its way back to more profitable neighborhoods. The advantage of the billy club, he soon found, was that the beggars and hawkers who would normally have approached a well-britched swell kept out of his way. He thought he might keep it. He thought briefly with a smile that it was what was needed to keep Amelia in line. But it was more likely she'd grab it and swing it at his head. In spite of his predicament, he laughed softly. He had walked a couple of miles before he finally saw a hack clip-clopping along with the air of having nowhere to go, and hailed it.

It was gone ten before he reached Albemarle Street, and when he walked in the front door, Bullock's eyes started out of his head.

"My lord!" he cried. "You! Here! But the race!"

"Precisely, Bullock. As you say, the race. Have the curricle brought round immediately and bring me a sandwich and a glass of porter from the kitchen. Quickly! And put this away somewhere." He handed him the cudgel.

"But my lord! Miss Moreton took the curricle. She said she was meeting you on Clapham Common. She said she'd had a note from you! I'm sorry, my lord. I didn't think to question her."

The Earl took in this astounding news with a sangfroid that demonstrated a breeding going back to William the Conqueror. "Of course you didn't," he said. "Who would dare? There has obviously been some misunderstanding." He paused a moment, "Tell them to saddle Wayfarer. I think he's the fastest. But don't forget the sandwich and porter. I'm famished."

"Porter, sir?" the poor old butler had never known his employer drink this humble potation except on the rare occasions he had a hangover. Could that be the problem? Could he be bosky so early in the day? Is that why he'd missed the start of the race?

"Yes, don't stand there gaping. And quickly."

Bullock tottered away, beginning to think the world was coming to an end.

It was close to eleven when the Earl emerged from his front door. He had had his riding jacket brushed while he ate a substantial beef sandwich and drank a mug of porter. He had been unable to find his tall curly-brimmed beaver and his many-caped riding duster. He did not mention this, but merely told his valet to find alternatives.

"By the way," he said to the groom holding his gleaming black saddle horse. "Did Miss Moreton take Tom?"

"Yes, my lord," came the reply.

"Of course she did," the Earl laughed. "Oh Amelia, Amelia, what have I done to deserve you?" he said under his breath, and leaped onto his horse.

Chapter Twenty-Four

Amelia had arrived at 23 Albemarle Street shortly after eight o'clock to find the racing curricle in front of the door and the household in a state of confusion. Bullock was wringing his hands and shouting at the head groom, who claimed he's sent his lordship's second team down to Crawley as directed two days before, and the last he had seen of his lordship was before eight o'clock that morning. The housekeeper was wailing that his lordship hadn't eaten any of his breakfast, and Tom was running around crying, "He ain't 'ere! Where is 'e? We gotta be off!"

She clapped her hands and demanded to know what was going on.

"It's his lordship, Miss," replied Bullock in unusual agitation. "He has disappeared. He went to the stables before eight this morning and hasn't been seen since. As you know, he is due to engage in a race today. It can only be that he has met with disaster. Nothing else would have prevented him from being here."

"Nonsense," said Amelia, with a calm she was far from feeling, and improvising madly. "He has merely forgotten to tell you that... that I am to meet him at Clapham Common." She made a swift decision. "Come Tom, stop making such a fuss and get into the curricle. We must be off immediately if we are not to be late. And oh, he asked me to bring his hat, gloves and caped duster. He... he forgot them. Tom, please take them with you. Excuse me, I must collect my things."

She went into her office and found the coat she had left there, together with her reticule. She left her bonnet. She didn't need two. Then she went into the library and took two of the thickest volumes she could find. Thus loaded, she returned to the front hall.

"I... er have to do some research for his lordship. I am taking these with me," she said, as nonchalantly as she could. She handed the whole lot to Tom, and the groom helped her up into the curricle. The whip was ready in its holder. She took up the reins, clicked to the horses and they were off.

As soon as they were away from the residential areas of London, she reined in the horses and turned to Tom. "Now, Tom, you have to trust me. I don't know where his lordship is, but I know he would not willingly miss this race. I'm going to take his place." When Tom began to remonstrate she said , "No, just listen. I am going to put his lordship's coat over mine and put his hat low on my head. I shall sit on these books to make me appear taller. Give me one of your stockings and your neckcloth. I'm sorry to ask you, but I have no alternative. Do this for me, please, and don't argue."

"Lor' bless yer, Miss. I'd do anyfink fer you. 'Ere." He rolled down one of his black stockings and gave it to her, then unwound his neckcloth.

Amelia removed her bonnet and stuffed it under the seat of the curricle. She put the two large books under her and covered them with her navy- blue coat. How glad she was it was such a gloomy color! She put his lordship's driving cloak over the coat she was wearing, but was forced to roll up the sleeves. She hoped the too-large gloves would cover them. She would remove his lordship's gloves and just wear her own as soon as they were underway. She wouldn't be able to feel the horses' mouths with the over-large ones on her hands. She pulled Tom's stocking over her bright curls and ruthlessly tucked them inside.

"Can you see my curls?" she asked Tom. He shook his head, so she put on his lordship's duster, turned up the collar and wound Tom's neckcloth around it all. When she put on his lordship's tall, curly-brimmed beaver, her face was almost totally obscured. "What do you think?" she asked her young companion. He grimaced expressively and shrugged his shoulders.

"I just have to stay as far away from everyone as I can. We're late, so there'll be no time for chatting, thank goodness. Just try to act naturally. Come on Tom, we can do this!"

She drove them at a good clip to Clapham Common, where a large crowd was gathered. She drove up around to where she could see Munson's curricle and the greys standing, waiting. She made a broad gesture with her left hand and then pointed at her throat, and gave a thumbs down, as if to indicate she had a sore throat. She hoped this would excuse her for not talking. Indeed, a couple of people she supposed to be his lordship's cronies came towards her, but she held out her hand, wearing the too-big gloves and pointed at her throat, shaking her head. They muttered amongst themselves but came no closer. Lord Smithson, who had been congratulating himself on Ailesbury's non-arrival, goggled when he saw his curricle drive up, with him in it. But when he made as if to approach, Tom jumped down and warded him off, saying "Don't 'ee come no closer, sir. Me lord's thinks 'e's got the beginnin' of a putrid sore throat. One o' the maids got it and fair poorly, she is. They was thinkin' she might stick 'er spoon in the wall. Best keep away."

Lord Smithson was no braver than the next man when it came to the mysterious illnesses that carried people off when they least expected it. He came no closer, contenting himself with the reflection that, at worst, if he was feeling poorly, Ailesbury would lose the race, and at best, he might die.

Last minute betting was fast and furious, especially when word got around that the Earl was feeling poorly. The odds swung heavily in favor of Munson, and when at last the flag was dropped to begin the race, they were running at 20-1 against his lordship.

Both drivers set off at a good clip, yet saving their horses for the climbs they knew they had ahead. Neither had used the road before but both had studied it. Munson had not thought it ungentlemanly, since he knew the Earl was more familiar with the route. Amelia had done so because she was naturally interested in where her employer was going. She had looked at the maps in the library and asked him about it. They had discussed the route, so she felt she knew what to do. She would have to keep the horses steady and not too fast through Streatham and Croydon so they would be ready for the rise through the Caterham Valley gap in the North Downs. If Munson was ahead of her there, she would overtake him on the hill. Then they could have their heads on the fairly straight run into Crawley. After changing horses at Crawley she would nurse them through the rise of the South Downs and let them out again into Brighton. She was confident in her own skill and she could already feel the speed of the lightweight racing curricle.

It would be important for Tom to be ready with the yard of tin to signal their arrival at tollgates of which there were many along the route. These tolls, while they were the bane of the traveler's existence, were responsible for the much-improved condition of the roads. Amelia just hoped she had enough money in her reticule to pay for them all, and gave her slim purse to Tom, so he would be ready when the time came. In the event, he proved very adept at dealing with the toll keepers, chaffing them with his cockney slang and not allowing a moment to be lost.

Amelia allowed Munson to take the lead at first, judging that the more he pushed his horses now, the less energy they would have later, especially as he alone, even without his tiger, was heavier than she and Tom combined. He was slower at the tolls, too. So as the Caterham Valley gap began to rise, she did as she had planned. She cracked the whip, and catching the thong in her gloved hand, urged the chestnuts into a full gallop. She swept past her opponent, and apart from steadying them to a slower pace on the descent, kept them at full tilt all the way into Crawley. Here, his lordship's second pair were quickly poled up while Amelia and Tom were offered a tankard of home brew. She was thirsty, but in her disguise, could hardly ask for a cup of tea, so she accepted it. In spite of her frown, so did Tom.

"Bless yer, Miss!" he said, "I bin drinking ale since I were a babe. Mother's milk it is to me!"

Knowing his background, she could well believe it. She took a couple of gulps from the tankard and found it bitter, but quite refreshing.

The horses were just ready, when a swirl of dust announced the arrival of Munson. They thrust the tankards at the ostlers, Amelia took up the reins, felt for the horses' mouths and they were off again. Out of Crawley there was a fairly steep climb into the South Downs, and Amelia kept the pair to a trot. It wasn't long before she heard Munson behind her and realized he was coming up fast with the fresh horses. Sure enough, he galloped by her in a cloud of dust.

"'E's gettin' ahead, Miss!" cried Tom. "Why're you goin' so slow?"

"It's a long climb," she replied calmly. "He can't keep up that pace. Don't worry."

A few miles later, in the village of Peas Pottage, she saw her chance. It turned out to be market day and Munson had been forced to slow his horses due to the press of vehicles in the tiny town center. He was vainly trying to maneuver around two gigs and several farm carts, but his blowing horses were uncomfortable with this turn of events. One minute they had been at a full gallop, then they'd been abruptly reined in and now were being jostled on both sides. Into the mix ran a dog who had succeeded in pulling a string of sausages from a butcher's cart. The butcher was giving chase, brandishing a large knife. Munson's horses took fright and stood, tossing their heads, refusing to move in any direction.

Amelia proceeded to demonstrate what an iron wrist and complete control can do. She kept her pair to a trot and skillfully skirted the jam of gigs, carts, dogs and butchers until she could see a clear space. It was not more than an inch wider than the curricle on either side, but Amelia trotted through it as if it were Bond Street on a Sunday afternoon. Leaving the town at a good trot, they breasted the top of the hill. Then she allowed her pair a full gallop until they began the descent on the other side. After that, Munson never saw more than the back of her head in the distance.

They had been on the road over three hours by now and Amelia's arms and back were tired. Sitting up on the books was very uncomfortable and though the curricle was well sprung, the trotting had been very hard on her spine. It was also very hot. The midday sun blazed down from a cloudless sky as it will sometimes do in Sussex in May. Wearing two coats and the stocking on her head underneath an ill-fitting hat had given her a headache. But, she thought, they must be two thirds of the way there, so perhaps only an hour or so to go. She could do it. She would do it. She gritted her teeth and concentrated on the horses, not herself.

As she came into Brighton, Amelia drew in the horses. She had been giving some thought as to how she was going to descend from the curricle and disappear. She guessed there would be a crowd at the Chapel Royal and they would be looking forward to a galloping finish.

"Listen, Tom," she said, "I'm going to trot along here until I see Munson arriving, and when he draws up just behind I'm going in at full gallop. I'm sure he'll do the same, but I won't let him overtake me. I want you get down and run to the Chapel Royal. It's just down there. I'll take the curricle past where the crowd is. I want you to be ready and the minute you see Munson gallop in, make one of the horses rear up. Between Munson arriving and the commotion I should be able to slip off on the side. I'll leave his lordship's hat, gloves and coat next to the curricle, pull off the stocking and pretend to be one of the crowd. Do you understand what I mean?"

Tom nodded earnestly, his eyes fixed on her face. Amelia continued urgently, "if anyone asks where the Earl is, say he was feeling unwell and ran off to cast up his accounts. You don't know where he is. As soon as you can, take the curricle and his things to the White Horse Inn and say he'll be along presently. I bespoke luncheon in a private room for him when I was organizing things for him. Put his coat and hat in the room and deal with the horses. Get yourself a dinner. Don't worry about payment. It will be on his lordship's account. Act normally. If they ask where he is, say you don't know, which is nothing more than the truth. Just stay there. I don't want anyone to see me here in case they suspect something. I'm going back to London. I'm sure his lordship will come if he can. If he doesn't show up, send word to Ailesbury House. I'll send a groom to help you bring back the curricle and the pair. You'll have to pick up the chestnuts in Crawley."

"Lor' 'elp yer, Miss," he protested, "I can do on me own. Them horses is like bruvvers to me!"

Amelia smiled. "We haven't got time to discuss it now! Go quickly! Munson will be here soon!"

Tom hopped down and ran off in the direction Amelia had indicated. She turned the curricle around and went back the way she had come. When she saw down the road a cloud of dust indicating a vehicle being ridden a speed, she turned again and started trotting briskly back towards the town center, for all the world as though she had just arrived. Judging to a nicety the speed at which Munson was approaching, she urged her pair into a gallop just as he arrived behind her. She kept herself just in front of him as she wheeled through the town and past the front of the Chapel Royal. The crowd cheered as the splendid sight of his lordship's curricle, easily recognizable by the crest on the sides, arrived at full gallop, the whip circling in the air.

As she had told Tom she would, she drew up just beyond where the crowd was enjoying the spectacle. People began to run towards her, but as they did, two things happened simultaneously. Munson also arrived at a gallop, and her outside horse reared up, pawing the air and neighing frantically. What Tom did or said to the horse she would never know, but the effect was to keep the crowd at bay and divert their attention from her.

196

Munson drew up closer to the front of the Chapel Royal. Amelia was able to push the books she had been sitting on to the floor of the curricle, grab her bonnet and reticule from under the seat and slip down to the ground. She quickly dropped his lordship's cloak, hat and gloves, threw Tom's neckcloth on top, pulled the stocking off her head, jammed her bonnet on her head and walked around towards the crowd.

Circling the outside of the milling spectators, Amelia was able to pass unremarked. She walked as swiftly as she could into the center of town. She was fearfully hot and thirsty, her back was hurting and she had a headache. The relief from pulling off the stocking and his lordship's hat, though, was enormous. Her head was hot, her curls stuck down with sweat. In spite of several curious glances, she removed her bonnet for a few minutes and allowed the fresh sea air to circulate around her head. It felt wonderful. Before long, her curls began to spring up in their usual way and she felt compelled to put her bonnet back on, for fear of being once again thought a madwoman. Walking gradually relieved the pain in her back and by the time she arrived in the center of town, she felt that if she could just have a cup of tea, she might feel her normal self.

But first she needed to find the time and place of departure of the next Stage back to London. She had heard there were about four a day in the warmer weather, not to mention the Royal Mail. But that most likely didn't leave till after dark and it would be much more expensive. By dint of asking her way of a couple of respectable-looking older women, she found that the Stage left from the Old Ship Inn on King's Road and arrived at the Blossoms Inn in Cheapside.

"But indeed, Miss," said one of the women, "That's no place for a girl like you after dark. My cousin Molly's girl who lives in

London came down from there last summer. She said it used to be called," and she whispered "Bosom's Inn, on account of the... well, the women that plied their trade there."

"Have no fear, Ma'am," replied Amelia. I shall immediately take a hackney away from it."

She thanked them and walked along the seafront to the Old Ship. There she was able to procure a seat on the Stage leaving in just over an hour, at three in the afternoon. The payment for this drastically depleted nearly all her remaining finances. Payment for a cup of tea and a bite to eat took the rest. The landlord took her money but shook his head and said they were mighty busy with people a-coming and a-going because of the road race – had she heard about it? But if she would take a seat in the room reserved for ladies, he would see what he could do to serve her before the Stage left.

The room turned out to be crowded and stuffy, and Amelia had to wait nearly the whole hour before the sustenance she had ordered materialized. She barely had time to drink the tea and take a bite of bread and cheese before the departure of the Stage was announced. Knowing she had no money left to buy anything later, she folded the remaining bread and cheese in her handkerchief and stuffed it in her reticule which by now was very much the worse for wear. She boarded the Stage, and by dint of looking haughtily down her nose at anyone who challenged her, took a seat by the window. She removed her bonnet, thankfully leaned her head against the none too clean squabs, and with a breeze on her face from the window she had been permitted to open a crack, fell asleep.

Chapter Twenty-Five

The Earl cursed as he rode through the thick London traffic of a late Wednesday morning. It seemed to him the streets were teeming more than usual with gigs, tilburies, barouches, curricles, carriages, hackneys and horsemen like himself, their progress made even slower by the multitude of street hawkers and vendors offering everything from caged canaries to meat pies. He was forced at times to go at little more than a walk. Every time he urged his horse into a trot, it seemed, his way would be barred by a large, slow barouche containing two or three elderly ladies who looked askance at his burst of speed.

Finally leaving the center of the metropolis behind, he was able to make better time, and he set his face firmly towards Brighton. It was not one of his favorite places at the best of times. Since the Prince Regent had chosen to take what had been a fairly modest palace and turn it into his summer retreat, it had become unbearably crowded in the warm weather. He was even now adding to it, making it more fanciful even than before. With him had come the inevitable hangers-on: people who wanted to be seen with him, and those who wanted to be seen with them. It had become almost impossible to hire a house for the season. All the best places were, of course, along the sea front. Though the outlook might be pleasant, the noise from the street and the curiosity of passers-by peering in one's windows, were not. On the whole, the Earl preferred to spend the summer at Deering in the shade of the ancient oaks and chestnuts.

Like Amelia, he changed horses in Crawley. Unlike her, he had a free run through Peas Pottage, market day being over for the week. However, the horse he had picked up was a slug, a far cry from his big hunter. Between this and the time he'd lost in the London traffic, he made up none of the two hours he was behind her. It was while he was cursing through his teeth on the uphill outside Crawley that she was galloping into the Chapel Royal yard, and by the time he arrived in Brighton, after nearly five hours on the road, she had boarded the Stage and was on her way back to London.

He rode straight to stables at the back of the White Horse Inn, relinquished the slug, hoping never to lay eyes upon him again, and there beheld his second pair of horses, peaceably munching their fodder. A quick look around confirmed that his curricle was there too. He was on his way to look for Miss Moreton when he was accosted by Munson.

"Ailesbury!" he said, clapping him on the back. "There you are! How's your throat? Looked for you all over, but that Tiger of yours said you were feeling queer and had taken yourself off. You look in fine fettle now. By God! What a race! I thought I had you once or twice, but after Peas Pottage, it was all over. It was worth losing to see the way you threaded that vehicle of yours through that crowd! An honor to lose to you, sir, an honor!" And he clapped him on the back again.

After that, it seemed there were innumerable well-wishers who desired to ask how he was feeling, shake his hand, discuss the race, ask what his plan had been, offer to buy him a drink, and give him the intelligence that his time had been only ten minutes over the record for the race, set a couple of years earlier by the Prince Regent himself. It seemed to him a lifetime before he could politely brush them all off and find the private room Amelia had booked for him.

After seeing to the appropriate stabling and treatment of his lordship's horses, Tom had engaged in a brief altercation with the landlord who did not recognize Lord Ailesbury's tiger and was not inclined to believe a word he said. It is true that the argument might have been more rapidly over had either of them fully understood the other. Tom was at his broadest cockney and the landlord, Sussex born and bred, at his most countrified. They could have been trying to converse in Chinese and Hindustani. It was solved in the end by Tom plunking himself down in the private room with his employer's caped duster and hat on his lap and refusing to move.

He was still there when the Earl strode in well over an hour later.

"Tom! Where's Ameli... Miss Moreton?"

"Gorn, sir. Back to Lunnon."

"Good God! Didn't she even have luncheon?"

"No, me lord. Told me to come 'ere an' wait for you. She was going back. Didn't want no one to see 'er."

Then he burst out, "You shoulda seen 'er, me lord! She sat up on a pile o'books and wore your 'at and cloak. Wiv me neckcloth round her phiz, 'er own mother wouldn't 'ave reckernized 'er! And to see 'er 'andle them 'orses! Ain't never bin nothing like it!"

"I hear you were only ten minutes off the record."

"Ten minutes off!" scoffed Tom! "Only acoz she stopped afore the Chapel Royal! She waited for 'im to catch up and then went on in cracking the whip like the blazes. She 'ad me get one o' the 'orses all riled up, so between 'im with 'is 'ooves in the air and Munson gallopin 'in be'ind 'er, she could slip orf and run away. An' that's wot she done! If yer arsk me, if she'd gorn straight in she'd 'ave beat that record fair 'n square!"

The Earl shook his head in amazement. "What a wonderful woman!" he said. "Well, I'm going after her. I hope they've got something better in the stables than that slug I came in on." He went to the door and called for the landlord.

"Find me a pair that can do more than walk all the way to London," he said. "and have them poled up to my curricle. And bring me something to eat, quickly. Some cold meat and a piece of bread will do. And I'll have a tankard of your home-brew."

"But, my lord," stammered the landlord. "Your luncheon? It's been ready these last two hours and more. A nice capon, as beautiful a piece of cod as you've ever laid eyes on, a dish of ...."

"No time," interrupted his lordship. "Tom, have you eaten?"

"No, sir, been waitin' for you."

The Earl turned to the landlord. "Give my luncheon to the boy and put it on my bill. All of it, mind! I owe him a great deal. And give him a room for the night. I'll send my groom first thing tomorrow. They can bring the horses home."

"Can't I come with you now, if you's leavin, me lord? An' I don't need no groom!" protested Tom.

"No, I want to go alone," responded his employer. "And I believe you could manage without a groom. But if anything should happen to you, it will blight whatever chance I have with Miss Moreton. Do me a favor. Do as I ask!"

"I wonder," he said to himself a little while later as he consumed yet another beef sandwich and swallowed a few mouthfuls of beer, "if I ask her to marry me, am I destined to eat this way the rest of my life? It's entirely possible I shall be reprimanded for my self-indulgent luncheons. That is, of course, when she's not telling me I spend too much on my boots, or complaining I let Antoine drink too much from my cellars, or, in her milder moments, proclaiming she wishes I'd break my neck or drown. But," he concluded with the last swallow, "it will be worth it. I'm sorry, Antoine. You may have to go."

With that, he bid farewell to his faithful servitor Tom, who sitting in his lordship's place, being waited on at his lordship's table, proceeded to enjoy a meal he would talk about for the rest of his life.

The horses he had been provided with were a reasonable pair, though the Earl was not tempted to add them to his stable. Nevertheless, he made good time. The Stage, even with four good horses, was very much slower than the curricle and pair, and it stopped frequently to allow passengers off and on. Amelia was glad of her rather mangled bread and cheese, and, like his lordship, began to wonder whether she would ever eat properly again. They were stopped in the village of Nutley when he caught up with her. She had descended from the coach to stretch her legs, leaving her bonnet on her seat. The sun was setting after the glorious day and the golden rays turned her hair to molten fire.

She felt, rather than heard, someone come up behind her, a someone who said, "You look like a goddess standing there with that glow all around you."

She spun around and before she could stop herself, threw herself against the Earl's broad chest. "Oh, my lord! I'm so glad you're all right!" she cried. "I knew the only thing that could stop you taking part in that race was if someone forcibly prevented you! I was so afraid you'd been injured!"

She suddenly realized what she was doing, and made as if to step back, but two strong arms prevented her. "But you told me you wished I would break my neck or drown," said his lordship, "and if you persist in calling me my lord, I shall drown myself." He pulled her even closer and nuzzled her hair. "Oh, Amelia, my adorable red-haired hornet, will you marry me?"

"M... marry you, my lo...? Oh," she cried in frustration, trying to disentangle herself, "what am I to call you? I can't call you Ned."

"Why not? Everyone else does. But call me anything you like, just marry me! And stop struggling, I'm not letting you go until you say yes."

"You can't marry me just because I took your place in a race to Brighton!" She looked up at him.

"It's exactly because you took my place in a race to Brighton that you must marry me. Just imagine if it were to get out that we were together at the White Horse Inn! And to compound it, I'm going to drive you to London all alone in the dark. Your reputation will be ruined. Don't you see, the only answer is for us to get married."

"No one cares a fig about my reputation. No one knows me. And why should the truth about the race get out? I was very careful that no one see me."

"But unless you're there to show me how to go on and what to say, who knows what I may let slip? You know what a useless fellow I am. Besides, I love you. I think I've loved you since the moment I saw you, but after you so magnificently told me to go to the devil, I was sure of it."

At this declaration, Amelia didn't know whether to laugh or cry.

Luckily, the coach driver chose that moment to announce, "All aboard! Leavin' in two minutes! Take yer seats ladies n' gentlemen!"

The Earl called back, "Miss Moreton is not going on. She's coming with me."

The scandalized faces of all the women travelers were immediately turned towards the pair, and mutters of "... no better than she should be...," could be heard distinctly.

"You see," said his lordship, turning back to Amelia, still tightly held in his arms. "I told you! Your reputation is quite lost, and just to make sure," he bent and kissed her lingeringly on the lips.

Amelia pushed him away at last, and laughed. "Well, if that's truly the case, I suppose I must marry you... Ned."

They watched as the coach driver whipped up his horses and, with a great clatter, left the inn yard.

Amelia exclaimed suddenly, "My bonnet! I left it in the coach!"

"Good," said the Earl. "All your bonnets are a positive disgrace. I shall purchase you new ones. As you know, buying presents for my lady loves is something I'm quite good at."

And they walked arm in arm, laughing, towards his lordship's curricle.

Chapter Twenty-Six

The next morning, the Earl sent his coach to pick up his intended, for, as he said when he left her at her door the night before, although she was a woman of no reputation, she was the future Countess of Ailesbury, and had a position to maintain. When she arrived at Albemarle Street, it was clear the whole household knew of their betrothal. Bullock threw the door open and bowed with enormous solemnity, and the whole staff crowded into the hall to present their astonished felicitations. It was hard for them to reconcile the woman who had regularly taken her lunch in the kitchen and who discussed with the maids the best way of lighting the fires, with the woman who was to be the Countess. Though, as Mrs. Hancock remarked, who better to become its mistress than the woman who knew absolutely everything about the house?

When his lordship tried to interfere with her morning perusal of his letters and invitations by pulling her to her feet and kissing her, she not too convincingly pushed him away, saying she was too busy for such interruptions. After all, she had three days' worth of work to attend to and so did he.

"You must write to your mother before the announcement goes in the newspapers," she said. "I don't think she'll be very pleased. When I was at Deering I convinced her I thought you were a frivolous fool."

"I know, she told me." The Earl laughed. "But when she sees what a man you've made of me, inducing me to give speeches in the house and propose legislation and lord knows what else, she'll love you as much as I do."

"Hmm." Amelia was doubtful. "I made her believe I like fencing and tennis more than giving dinner parties. Actually I do, but I promise I'll be a conformable wife and do as I ought."

"A conformable wife?" the Earl burst into laughter. "Now, that I shall never believe! And I sincerely hope you won't be. If I'd wanted a dull wife I could have married any of the simpering virgins thrust at me these last five years and more. No, my love. I'm marrying a hornet, and we both know it."

Amelia pretended to ignore him. "I must write to Aurelius. He should know before anyone else. In fact, because he's head of the family, you should ask his permission to pay me your addresses! How funny!" and she too went off into a peal of laughter.

Then her reluctant betrothed had to admit to his subterfuge in getting Aurelius to agree to let him pay for the Commission.

"You mean you told him we were going to be married, even before you asked me?" she said in utter disbelief.

"Yes, well, my love, I had to say something. A man's not going to let a virtual stranger pay his debts and buy him a Commission. You have to see that."

"Wait a minute – you paid his debts too?"

"Of course! Someone had to! Smithson was dunning him, you see. That was his first attempt to discredit us, well, you. Then he moved on to me."

On the way home from Brighton he had told her about his adventure in the cellar and who was behind it.

"The man's a menace! What can be done about him?" Then, coming back to the matter at hand, Amelia exclaimed, "You told Aury we were going to be married! But what if I'd refused you?"

"Well, I told him you might, but he said you'd been in love with me from the start. He knew because you didn't talk about me and colored up if anyone mentioned my name."

"I didn't... I don't..., well, I do, I am, but... that's ridiculous," said Amelia in confusion, and her betrothed was forced to kiss her again because he found it adorable that she should, for once, be at a loss for words.

When that agreeable interlude was over, he murmured in her ear, "Don't worry about Smithson. I've something in mind."

In fact, a day later the Earl found Lord Smithson finishing his lunch at White's. He first had to run another gauntlet of back slapping and congratulations from the many members who had bet on his winning, and reluctant admiration from those who had not.

"Smithson!" he announced heartily, coming into the dining room. "I'd be obliged if you let me sit with you a moment."

The other man looked as if he'd be much happier if the Earl went somewhere else, but nodded gracelessly.

"I hope you're not too much out of pocket over the race," he said in the friendliest way possible. "I heard you wagered heavily on Munson."

"No," returned the other with a weak smile. "I... er, had a little flutter, that's all."

"Good, good! Glad to hear it!" replied the Earl, knowing it was a complete lie. "Just a little fun, that's all it was!"

He was silent for a moment. Then he continued. "But the curious thing is, someone actually tried to keep me from taking part in it. You might not believe it, but I was hit over the head in front of my home and put in a cellar by two thugs. Now, what were their names? Ah yes, I remember! Albert and Bernard, or Bernie, was it? Yes, I rather think it was. Bernie was the owner of the cudgel. My butler has it now. You will be astonished when I tell you the cellar I was held in was under your premises down on the Thames. Since they asked for no ransom, and did not even pick my pockets, I can only assume their aggression was for no other purpose than to keep me from the race. But the silly fellows tripped over their own feet and fell in a heap, so I was able to make good my escape. The blow over the head did make me feel a little unwell, I admit, but the fresh sea air of Brighton soon put me to rights."

He was silent again, letting this sink in. "I am on my way to lodge the information with the Bow Street Runners. I'm sure that they will soon be able to identify my attackers and find out who put them up to it. No one will believe such uncouth fellows did it on their own account. And the newspapers will no doubt also find it a thrilling story." He got up to leave.

But Lord Smithson raised a hand to stop him. "Er… Ailesbury," he said, hesitating. "I… well, I'm exceedingly sorry it should have been my… er, my cellar. You don't need to go to so much… er trouble. I'll look into it myself. Bow Street Runners, you know. But in the meantime, if I may be of… er, service to you, I should be very… er, very happy."

"My good man, I'm touched! That is most gracious!" exclaimed the Earl, sitting down again. "As a matter of fact, there is something. As you know, I made my Maiden Speech on the subject of the conditions of non-apprenticed workers in our factories. As a mill owner, this is a topic that touches you most nearly. If you would give your vocal support to the Bill I propose to introduce, it would carry particular weight. May I count on you?"

Lord Smithson knew he was beaten. He had the choice of supporting legislation that would cost him money or having his name dragged through the mud of an investigation and the newspapers. He chose the former.

"Well," he said slowly. "I should be... er, yes, glad to support you, Ailesbury. I've been thinking myself it was time it was looked into. Yes. You can... er, count on me." He looked at the Earl rather with the look of a beaten dog who knew he had deserved it. "And... er, I'm happy your injuries were not more... er, serious."

"Thank you, Smithson!" replied his lordship. "That is most generous of you. It will help me twice over. But you must keep me informed of the progress of the investigation."

He stood, bowed his goodbye and left the club, very satisfied. "Don't know about Aurelius," he said to himself, "but I think I'm a loss to the Diplomatic Services myself. Damme if I don't see about a post!"

For the next few months, every time the Earl saw Smithson he kindly asked about the progress of the investigation. The Peer became so unhappy that he ceased frequenting the clubs. He had never been very popular and no one missed him.

212

Chapter Twenty-Seven

The Earl was right when he said his mother would change her mind about Amelia. She had read the report of his Maiden Speech with astonishment, and when he wrote to say he was betrothed to the woman who had forced him into making it, she did, indeed, think that extraordinary young woman might be the making of him. She was still a little worried about her ability to preside over one of the Great Houses of England, but when she appeared at Deering, a short time later, her mind was put at rest.

His lordship had dragged Amelia off to the most fashionable modiste in London, where he was well known for the payment of gowns for his previous *chères amies*. In that exclusive feminine enclave with mirrors on every wall, she submitted to being stripped to her shift, measured, considered and looked at from every angle. Then Madame had dropped everything to make the future Countess a full panoply of day dresses, afternoon dresses, walking dresses, evening gowns, ball gowns and even a new riding ensemble and hunting jacket. A visit to the most expensive milliner in town produced box after box of glorious bonnets. His lordship's only stipulation was they would not cover all his beloved's fiery curls. The hatmaker remarked to her junior that they couldn't have done so even if they had wanted to. Miss Moreton's hair had a mind of its own.

The result was that when Amelia and her betrothed went to Deering, they had to have a whole carriage come behind to carry her wardrobe. She laughingly protested until her fiancé told her he was damned if he would let his future wife be seen one moment longer in the rags she was wont to wear.

"You may bully me as much as you like, Miss Moreton," he said, "but in this I stand firm. The honor of the family is at stake. Since you put yourself at great risk protecting it once before, I cannot understand your reluctance to do so now, at no pain to yourself and at enormous pleasure to me."

What could she say? "Yes, my lord," she acquiesced meekly.

When the announcement of the betrothal appeared in the newspapers, the ton was astounded. Who was this Amelia Moreton? Was she related to that young Aurelius? Where was he, by the way? They hadn't seen him in an age. A couple of those more intimate with his lordship had heard talk of a female secretary, but had dismissed it as gossip. But now they remembered. It was soon known around town that yes, Ned Woodbridge was to marry his one-time member of staff. The exact nature of their relationship naturally gave rise to a good deal of comment.

But they reckoned without the combined powers of the betrothed couple to arrange a Ball of Introduction for Amelia. At the Earl's instruction, the ball was so dazzling, and the future Countess's demeanor so haughty as she met the two hundred guests from London's highest society that they immediately discarded the idea that she had ever been anything but a lady. The ball was on the 16th of June. Amelia herself arranged the printing of the invitations and booked the musicians. She arranged for link-boys for the host of carriages and contacted the Officer of the Watch to warn them of likely traffic jams. But it was the Earl who ordered the flowers and, with Monsieur Antoine, arranged a menu for the intimate dinner for 40 beforehand and the late supper for the whole company at two in the morning. It turned out that he was a dab hand at organizing things when he put his mind to it and more than once said, again, he was a loss to the Diplomatic Service. Since he had excellent taste in these matters and had been to innumerable balls over the years, he knew what he wanted. He got it.

No. 23 Albemarle Street had never looked so glorious, the company more sparkling nor the happy couple more stunning than that night. Her betrothed had insisted on and ordered for Amelia a scarlet gown, because, as he said, the sight of her in her hunting jacket was seared forever in his mind. It was of watered silk that glimmered in different shades with the light, and when combined with her fiery hair was enough to dim the thousands of candles placed in every niche in the house. The gown was low over the bosom and the tiny puff sleeves and skirt were trimmed with seed pearls. The only jewelry Amelia wore was her mother's pearl necklace. She had accepted the services of a dresser proposed by Mrs. Hancock who had drawn her abundant curls up onto the top of her head with ringlets falling artistically around her ears. She was radiant.

The Earl was dressed in the customary black satin knee britches with white stockings and waistcoat, and a waisted swallow-tail coat. His neckcloth was a thing of perfection, held in place by a single ruby headed pin. But though his clothing was customary, the fit was not. His coat looked molded to his frame, and his britches were without a wrinkle. Amelia couldn't resist kissing him and telling him he was easily the best-looking man present. But, of course, she said, that's because Aurelius wasn't there.

In fact, it was a good thing she didn't know what Aurelius was doing that night of the 16th of June. He was bivouacking on the plain on Mont-Saint-Jean close to the village of Waterloo after riding with his company all day in the pouring rain. Wellington had ordered a strategic retreat towards the sloping ground outside the village he had identified a year before as the best place in Belgium for his tactics. Lord Uxbridge's Hussars, including Aurelius Moreton, had fought a rear-guard action from the town of Quatre Bras in Belgium. The British Army was preparing for battle.

The next day, Wellington called for a group of Hussars to reconnoiter the French positions on the road to Namur and discover the whereabouts of the allied Prussian troops. Aurelius volunteered. After several hours' ride and threading their way perilously though a number of French outposts, the scouting party discovered that the French were holding the Namur Road. Aurelius distinguished himself by volunteering to draw the enemy's fire so the rest of the company could go forward. He lay still long enough for the French to think he was dead before wriggling backwards on his belly, finding his horse and continuing on. They confirmed that the French were making no attempt to advance. Bonaparte was apparently enjoying a late breakfast. Finally, they located the Prussian troops on the high ground above the road. They returned and reported this to Wellington. Satisfied that he could fight from his position in Waterloo if the Prussians would send just two corps to help him, the British General laid out the disposition of his troops.

The following day, the 18th of June 1815, was a day that would live forever in British history. By a brilliant combination of tactics and effrontery in which he disguised the position and strength of his men from the French General, and by the lucky arrival of the Prussians in the nick of time, Wellington won the Battle of Waterloo. Aurelius's Hussar regiment distinguished itself by its tenacity, even though Lord Uxbridge lost a leg in the engagement. The outcome of the battle was for a long time by no means a foregone conclusion. According to reports that later filtered into London, it could have gone either way. But several things were clear: before the battle, the Hussars under Uxbridge had materially helped Wellington by performing a model rear-guard action. Then, by their repeated charges on the field of battle they had significantly contributed to the victory. And one Aurelius Moreton, promoted to Captain on the spot, was a hero.

By the beginning of August, the Captain was back in London. He had been mentioned in dispatches; his future in the Hussars was rosy. He was invited to the Palace for a Commendation and medals. He was as handsome as ever, in fact, even more so in his regimentals. He was invited everywhere. Young women flocked to his side. Men in the clubs listened to his accounts of events at Waterloo as if he were a sage. Even if Smithson had wanted to try to bring up the old business of the gambling debts, no one would have listened to him. But the thing that made him happiest was to be reunited with his sister. She and the Earl had delayed their wedding until he could be there to walk Amelia down the aisle.

"You know, Amy," he said to her the day before her wedding. "It's a good thing I was stupid enough to get into trouble and had to be helped out by Ned, because you would never have let me go. And by God, I'm glad I went! But," he said after a pause, "you were always with me. As I told you I would, I always asked myself: would Amy do this? And if the answer was no, I didn't. I knew you'd let those Frogs fire at you so the others could get away. You used to do that when we were little. Take the fire for me. I bet you'd do the same for Ned."

"Oh, I already did," she said, and told him all about the race.

Edward Woodbridge, Earl of Ailesbury, third Baron of Mayne and Miss Amelia Moreton were married in Westminster Abbey on 15th August. It was a glorious day with the slightest of wispy clouds high in the sky. Everyone present declared they had never seen a happier or more handsome couple. After a wedding breakfast that began at noon and ended at four, the Earl and Countess left for a protracted trip on the Continent, now free once again of Napoleon Bonaparte. To be sure, it wasn't the best time of year to travel, but, declared Ned, he had to be back for the opening of Parliament in October. After all, he had responsibilities. His wife just smiled.

Epilogue

Towards the end of 1815, the Earl's call for improvement of conditions for children working in factories received unexpected support from Robert Peel, a colleague and baronet. Nevertheless, in spite of their continued efforts, a Bill was only finally passed in 1819 and was considerably weaker than either of them wanted. However, over the following twenty years stronger legislation, together with the growth of public education, gradually improved the lives and opportunities of poor children in Britain.

The End

A Note from the Author

If you enjoyed this novel, please leave a review! Reviews are so important to independent authors like me! Go to the Amazon page and scroll down past all the other books Amazon wants you to buy(!) till you get to the review click.

https://www.amazon.com/Lord-Red-Headed-Hornet-GL-Robinson/dp/B08W3F1XH4/ref=tmm

For a free short story and to listen to me read the first chapter of all my Regencies, please go to my website:

https://romancenovelsbyglrobinson.com

Regency Novels by GL Robinson

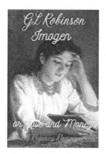

Imogen or Love and Money. Lovely young widow Imogen is pursued by Lord Ivo, a well-known rake. She angrily rejects him and concentrates on continuing her late husband's business enterprises. But will she find that money is more important than love?

Cecilia or Too Tall to Love. Orphaned Cecilia, too tall and too outspoken for acceptance by the *ton,* is determined to open a school for girls in London's East End slums, but is lacking funds. When Lord Tommy Allenby offers her a way out, will she get more than she bargained for?

Rosemary or Too Clever to Love. Governess Rosemary is forced to move with her pupil, the romantically-minded Marianne, to live with the girl's guardian, a strict gentleman with old fashioned ideas about young women should behave. Can she save the one from her own folly and persuade the other that she isn't just a not-so-pretty face?

The Kissing Ball. A collection of Regency short stories, not just for Christmas. All sorts of seasons and reasons!

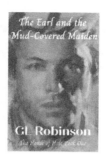

The Earl and The Mud-Covered Maiden. The House of Hale Book One. When a handsome stranger covers her in mud driving too fast and then lies about his name, little does Sophy know her world is about to change forever.

The Earl and His Lady. The House of Hale Book Two. Sophy and Lysander are married, but she is unused to London society and he's very proud of his family name. It's a rocky beginning for both of them.

The Earl and The Heir. The House of Hale Book Three. The Hale family has a new heir, in the shape of Sylvester, a handful of a little boy with a lively curiosity. His mother is curious too, about her husband's past. They both get themselves in a lot of trouble.

The Lord and the Red-Headed Hornet. Orphaned Amelia talks her way into a man's job as secretary to a member of the aristocracy. She's looking for a post in the Diplomatic Service for her twin brother. But he wants to join the army. And her boss goes missing on the day he is supposed to show up for a wager. Can feisty Amelia save them both?

The Lord and the Cat's Meow. A love tangle between a Lord, a retired Colonel, a lovely debutante and a fierce animal rights activist. But Horace the cat knows what he wants. He sorts it out.

The Lord and the Bluestocking The Marquess of Hastings is good-looking and rich but is a little odd. Nowadays he would probably be diagnosed as having Asperger's syndrome. To find a wife he scandalizes the ton by advertising in the newspaper. Elisabeth Maxwell is having no luck finding a publisher for her children's book and is willing to marry him to escape an overbearing step-father. This gently amusing story introduces us to an unusual but endearing Regency couple. The question is: can they possibly co-exist, let alone find happiness?

About The Author

GL Robinson is a retired French professor who took to writing Regency Romances in 2018. She dedicates all her books to her sister, who died unexpectedly that year and who, like her, had a lifelong love of the genre. She remembers the two of them reading Georgette Heyer after lights out under the covers in their convent boarding school and giggling together in delicious complicity.

Brought up in the south of England, she has spent the last forty years in upstate New York with her American husband. She likes gardening, talking with her grandchildren and sitting by the fire. She still reads Georgette Heyer.

Made in the USA
Las Vegas, NV
09 August 2023

75877570R00134